He really was very handsome. And full of personality and humor. The kind of man any woman would be excited and thrilled to be with.

The perfect date to bring to a wedding.

She stared at her reflection in the mirror and gave her head a shake. *Nah.* How would she even begin to ask him something like that? But what was the alternative? She didn't have any really close male friends. And as luck would have it, all her close female friends wouldn't be able to help, either. Rachel and Leigh were both only children. Carla had two sisters and Miranda's brother was overseas on active duty. Laney's only other option was to fess up to her family.

Plus...the plan wasn't without appeal. For one thing, she'd get a chance to see him again. Still, as far as ideas went, it was foolish and harebrained and impulsive.

But it just might work.

Dear Reader,

When the first inklings of Gianni and Laney's story appeared in my mind, I knew I would have to set their adventure in beautiful Italy. Though the two meet and start falling in love in Boston, a rather impromptu trip to the Amalfi Coast truly begins to drive their growing attraction and affection for each other.

But they don't make it easy on themselves. Gianni has a family history he's grappled with his entire life. A scandalous family secret has always left him feeling like an outsider in his own home. As for Laney, she's never been quite enough to earn her parents' approval and acceptance. Even though they have so much in common, the scars of disavowal from those they loved the most have made them both leery and distrustful. Neither wants to risk the potential hurt of yet another rejection. But their growing love proves too strong to ignore. Laney's discovery that she's expecting triggers a reckoning that begins the healing both she and Gianni need to move forward.

In each other, they finally find the true family they've longed for their entire lives. I hope you enjoy their journey.

Nina

From Wedding Fling to Baby Surprise

Nina Singh

Recycling programs for this product may not exist in your area.

ISBN-13: 978-1-335-40681-1

From Wedding Fling to Baby Surprise

This is a work of fiction. Names, characters, places and incidents are either the product of the author's imagination or are used fictitiously. Any resemblance to actual persons, living or dead, businesses, companies, events or locales is entirely coincidental.

This edition published by arrangement with Harlequin Books S.A.

For questions and comments about the quality of this book, please contact us at CustomerService@Harlequin.com.

Harlequin Enterprises ULC
22 Adelaide St. West, 40th Floor
Toronto, Ontario M5H 4E3, Canada
www.Harlequin.com

Printed in U.S.A.

Nina Singh lives just outside Boston, Massachusetts, with her husband, children and a very rambunctious Yorkie. After several years in the corporate world, she finally followed the advice of family and friends to "give the writing a go, already." She's oh-so-happy she did. When not at her keyboard, she likes to spend time on the tennis court or golf course. Or immersed in a good read.

Books by Nina Singh

Harlequin Romance

How to Make a Wedding

From Tropical Fling to Forever

Destination Brides

Swept Away by the Venetian Millionaire

9 to 5

Miss Prim and the Maverick Millionaire

The Marriage of Inconvenience
Reunited with Her Italian Billionaire
Tempted by Her Island Millionaire
Christmas with Her Secret Prince
Captivated by the Millionaire
Their Festive Island Escape
Her Billionaire Protector
Spanish Tycoon's Convenient Bride
Her Inconvenient Christmas Reunion

Visit the Author Profile page at Harlequin.com.

To all those who feel they are the odd ones.
May you find where you truly belong.

**Praise for
Nina Singh**

"A captivating holiday adventure!
Their Festive Island Escape by Nina Singh
is a twist on an enemies-to-lovers trope and
is sure to delight. I recommend this book to
anyone.... It's fun, it's touching and it's satisfying."

—*Goodreads*

CHAPTER ONE

"YOU'RE BREAKING UP with me?"

Laney Taytum stared at her phone screen as if it had grown tentacles since she'd answered its ring.

"And you're doing it over the phone? While you're across the country on business?"

Joseph's loud and long-suffering sigh could be heard clearly from the other end of the line.

He'd been her steady and serious boyfriend for the past two or so years.

A status that seemed to be about to change.

Surprisingly, the flush of emotion running through her right now couldn't exactly be described as hurt. More like a stinging sense of disappointment.

They'd never been that kind of couple—the hot-and-heavy, can't-keep-our-hands-off-each-other kind. She'd never really felt that spark that she so often read about in the paperbacks she picked up in the grocery checkout line. But they'd been comfortable with each other. Enough that her weekends weren't spent alone on the couch, eating a pint of Rocky Road.

Maybe not the most exciting setup, but she'd thought it was a beneficial arrangement for them both. Clearly, that had been a bit naive on her part.

"Don't do this, Laney," he said now. "You had to sense this was coming."

She had not.

"But my sister's wedding. The trip to Italy." How could he dump her at such a time? There was no doubt that they'd passed a point on the road that there'd be no turning back from.

Emily's wedding was the very next month, in two weeks to be specific. The trip she and Joseph had booked together was scheduled a couple of weeks after that. How quickly did Joseph think she could move on after their long-term relationship?

It occurred to her then that he probably already had.

Her favorite cousin's voice echoed in her head. *I'm not gonna lie to you, sweetie. He strikes me as a bit of a jerk.*

While the rest of her family gave the two of them the suggestive wink and nod about marriage, Mabel had never taken a shine to Joseph. Apparently, she was much wiser than the lot of them. To think, Laney had felt rather offended at Mabel's straightforwardness at the time.

Looked like she owed Mabel an apology.

And now Laney would have to break the news to them all. While they'd been expecting the announcement of an engagement, she'd instead be attending her sister's nuptials sans a plus-one.

"How will I tell everyone?" The question was more a thought posed out loud as she was trying to process.

Joseph was silent for a beat before he answered, "Your reaction kind of proves my point. I'll try not to take it too personally."

He was trying to not take things personally? Of all the… The man was the very definition of a jerk.

She went from shocked to irritated. Then angry.

"Take it any way you'd like." For the first time, Laney realized her voice sounded echo-like through the air. He must have had her on speaker. Was he even alone? "How exactly does my question prove your point?"

Perhaps he had the other woman in the room, eavesdropping, making sure he was going through with her dumping. She was probably listening to the whole conversation, egging him on.

Or maybe he was just a coward who didn't even have the guts to do this face-to-face.

"Darling," Joseph began, "I just told you I'm breaking up with you and your first response is to wonder how you're going to break the news to others. Kind of validates that we shouldn't be together."

Well, what did he expect her to do? Grovel? Cry? Tell him how hurt she was?

Before Joseph, her life had been a series of bad dates when she could find the time to break away from her responsibilities at the club. The two of them didn't always agree on everything, but she felt comfortable around him. Secure in the knowledge that she had a steady partner.

But she wasn't the type to do any kind of groveling or crying. Not since she was a child. Growing up in a family like hers, one didn't show emotion if one could help it. So she'd learned to keep hers in check.

For the most part, anyway.

"Aren't you even going to ask me why?" Joseph was now asking.

Like it mattered. Like it made any difference whatsoever.

Knowing his reasoning was not going to change the fact that she had all sorts of logistical and financial issues to now figure out, between the wedding and the trip.

Knowing his reasons wasn't going to change any part of this scenario. Still, she would humor him. Let him get it all off his chest.

"Tell me why, Joseph," she told him on a sigh.

He didn't hesitate to respond. "I'm bored,

Laney. I have been for quite some time. And you didn't even notice," he added with an accusing tone.

He was calling her *boring*?

She'd been fully prepared to hear him say they were incompatible, and that they wanted different things in life. She definitely had not anticipated the sudden direction of the conversation.

Before she could absorb it all fully, Joseph continued, "I mean, when was the last time you tried anything new? And I don't mean agreeing to go to the new Vietnamese place downtown."

Then what did he mean? Laney blinked in confusion. Was he referring to the bedroom? Was she being prudish with him? She hadn't really thought so. But clearly, she hadn't been paying attention.

"When your sister introduced us, she couldn't say enough about how unconventional you were. How different."

Ha! Laney wanted to laugh out loud. Different was relative. She was nothing like the rest of her family, so her sister hadn't been lying to him. Then Joseph threw the proverbial and very sharp dagger. "You're just not an exciting woman to be with."

Despite herself, Laney felt the sting of hurtful tears. While she'd seen their relationship as comfortable and easy, he had obviously found it dull and flat.

She'd been such a fool not to have seen it. In that, at least, he was right.

She had to move on past the hurt, focus on the current situation before her. Focus on the facts at hand.

"You owe me for the trip," she reminded him. "I paid for the booking of it up front."

They were supposed to go to Positano and Florence together two weeks after her sister's wedding. Another stab of hurt shot through her. During the planning, she'd assumed Joseph would take the opportunity to propose himself given the timing.

What a fool she was.

Joseph sighed. "About that. I have an offer for you."

Alarm bells went off in her head. Something told her she wasn't going to like this offer of his. "And what would that be?"

"I'm perfectly happy to pay for the whole trip and go without you."

Laney tried not to react. She'd suspected as much. He wanted to go with someone else. Despite the suspicion, his words served as a figurative punch to the gut. How long had he been deceiving her?

"Otherwise," Joseph continued, "I don't plan on paying you for my half. Take it or leave it. That's the only deal on the table."

She was right. She didn't like his *deal* one bit.

"Well, I happen to have a counteroffer. Feel free to drop dead!"

Disconnecting the call without waiting for a response, she took a deep breath and steadied herself. She had a long night ahead of her. Friday's were always busy enough at the club. The fact that this past week in Boston had been cloudy gray and rainy would ensure the usual crowd would be even larger with people looking to get out and party and dance.

Being the owner of a rather popular night spot meant she was in a packed dance club night after night, surrounded by a crowd of partyers. Hence, her rare evenings at home were particularly sacred. Especially on a day like this one, where all she wanted to do was lick her wounds.

As tempting as it was to call in and spend the evening at home in sweats and fuzzy socks, deep into that aforementioned pint of Rocky Road, she wouldn't do that to her staff.

Processing her breakup, including the fact that her boyfriend of two years had just told her she'd been boring him to tears, was just going to have to wait.

He had clearly just stepped into the seventh circle of Hades.

Gianni Martino scanned the crowded dance floor and bristled with impatience. This really wasn't his kind of scene. What a lousy way to spend a Saturday night. He'd much rather be back at the main gym working out or in the ring sparring with Mario. But that afternoon his father, Franco, had reminded him yet again that he still hadn't scoped out the latest site he had in mind for further expansion within the city.

Better to get this over with, and then he could go about his night the way he wanted. This place was going to need a lot of work. All around him, sweaty bodies gyrated and bounced to a resoundingly loud techno song that was ridiculously heavy on the bass, even for a dance song. He groaned aloud in frustration. How did people enjoy this? Although, he had to admit, the scantily clad and heavily made-up women on the dance floor certainly made for enticing eye candy. A couple feet away, a group of female club goers were darting glances his way and giggling to each other. He was accustomed to such attention. He knew he fell into the category of tall and dark, plus he worked for his family-owned chain of gyms, so he was naturally physically fit. A combination that tended to ensure he was never at a loss for female companionship.

He observed the women again. Large diamond studs adorned the ears of one. A sparkly designer watch graced the wrist of another. They were clearly fit and had money. Gianni thought about handing them all the Martino's free-pass gym coupons that he always carried with him.

One of the eye candies moved in his direction and stepped within inches of where he stood. He could smell the sharp, spicy scent of her perfume. Her brilliant blue eyes flashed at him and her smile widened into a grin.

"Please tell me you're here alone," she demanded in a breathless tone.

He thought about lying. Then decided there was no need. "I am."

She angled closer and pulled up against him, then grabbed him by the elbow. In a display of strength that somewhat took him by surprise, she yanked him closer to the dance floor. "Then you have to dance with me."

He stood firm after the first step. "I'm not much of a dancer, sweetheart."

She chuckled at that, clearly not deterred. If anything, she pressed closer up against him, skimmed her hand up his chest to his shoulder. "Then why are you here? This is the most popular dance club in Greater Boston."

There was no way he was going to get into all that with her. How exactly would he explain that he was actually here on business on a Friday night, just as the evening had begun?

She would never believe it.

He would then have to explain that he was

a senior VP at his family's company. Martino Entertainment Enterprises was a global entity, which owned everything from gaming halls to small casinos to fitness centers and boxing gyms. The latter being his very own idea and accomplishment.

"Maybe some other time," he told the woman with a friendly yet dismissive smile.

The woman gave him a mini shrug. "Well, I'll be here for a few more hours if you change your mind," she threw over her shoulder before walking away to rejoin her friends. Any other night, Gianni might have entertained the offer she'd not so subtly thrown at him. A romantic interlude without any attachments was sometimes just what a man—or a woman—needed. But he really was here on business. And he never mixed business with pleasure. It was the reason he was drinking nothing stronger than a cola at the moment.

After about fifteen minutes, he'd seen enough. Logistically, the place was exactly what they'd been looking for. The square footage, the setup of the building and geographical location made it perfect for acquisition. Everything else would need to be gutted.

He'd already surmised that he'd have to make the current owner a hefty offer, one they couldn't refuse. A lot of work and planning had clearly gone into the place. No doubt, it was professionally decorated—with avant-garde lighting and comfortable seating. The dance floor was large and highly polished. A wraparound bar heavily stocked with the highest grade of spirits and wine was currently mobbed with thirsty customers. Four professional dancers performed on an elevated stage in every corner, occasionally jumping off to wrangle those who appeared to be hesitant to enter the dancing fray.

All in all, Gianni figured he would have to commend the current proprietor. They'd done a nice job—created a welcoming, fun atmosphere. Everyone seemed to be having a good time.

Except one. His gaze fell on her at that very moment, right before he'd been getting ready to exit and go about his night. She walked past him carrying a tray of drinks and delivered it to what appeared to be a VIP table just a few feet away.

She looked utterly miserable.

The waitress uniform she had on—a black tuxedo vest and knee-length leather skirt—fit her to perfection. Her dark hair was piled high on top of her head with tendrils of curls framing her face. She looked more like a pop star about to go on stage than a cocktail waitress in a dance club. Even in the dark, her eyes were striking. An amber-gold shade of hazel that reminded him of a summer sunset.

When had he ever noticed a stranger's eyes before, let alone compared them to a sunset?

Gianni found himself unable to tear his gaze away as she handed out the drinks and made small talk, the smile on her face clearly forced and strained. Watching her made him more curious than he could explain.

Maybe she was just tired, maybe it had been a long night and her feet hurt in the lace-up, block-heeled black leather boots she was wearing.

The real question was, why did he want to know so badly?

CHAPTER TWO

She could feel his eyes on her.

And it was becoming harder and harder to ignore his gaze. Laney did her best to focus on the task at hand. All she had to do was deliver this tray of drinks, then head back for the next order. Then repeat.

Simple. She'd done it hundreds of times in the past. But tonight felt different. She'd begun her shift feeling out of sorts because of Joseph's cowardly phone call.

But her discomfort at the moment consisted of a whole other layer. She was beyond aware of the customer sitting alone at the table by the edge of the dance floor. He definitely wasn't a regular. She would have remembered a face like his. Dark, handsome in an angular, sharp-jawed kind of way. Not her usual type at all. The man was clearly fit. By contrast, Joseph had been fair and rather lanky. As were the few other men she'd dated over the years. Whereas this man couldn't be described as lanky at all. Probably not since junior high. Broad-shouldered with toned muscles visible through the long-sleeved Henley shirt he wore, he was the fittest specimen of a man she'd seen. And he seemed to carry it with an air of grace.

She'd never gone for muscular before. Nothing about this stranger should be calling to her in any way.

Why was he here alone? He didn't seem the type to often be lacking in female company.

Even as the thought ran through her mind, a tall statuesque blonde in mile-high stilettos strode over to him from the other side of the bar. That hadn't taken long at all. Laney hadn't thought he'd be standing there by himself for long, and she'd been right. She prepared herself for the show; the lady was no doubt ready to laser blast all her charm on the guy, who was probably all too willing to receive it. Only, upon closer inspection, the expression on the woman's face appeared less than flirtatious. In fact, she looked downright angry. Combative, even.

Before Laney could so much as process what was happening, the woman flung out her arm in a flash of movement. The next instant, the gentleman's shirt was soaked and his face dripping with the evening's cocktail special.

The woman had tossed her drink in his face!

She gave a final humph with a raise of her chin, then stomped back where she'd come from.

To his credit, he didn't react in any kind of anger or frustration. He didn't even look shocked, for that matter.

Laney faltered in her step. As proprietor of the establishment, she had to tend to her customers. All of them.

She made her way over to him, pulling out the tea towel from her apron's waistband. She handed it to him when she reached his side. Luckily, none of the liquid had made its way to the floor to cause any kind of slipping hazard. Or rather unluckily in his case, it had all landed squarely on his person.

"Thanks," he uttered, wiping his face and neck.

"No problem."

He did the best he could with the towel before handing it back to her.

"Just one question," she began, seemingly unable to help herself.

He shrugged. "Sure. Why not?"

"Did you deserve it?"

He had the gall to wink at her before answering, "Probably."

"Go ahead and laugh," Gianni prompted. His skin felt sticky everywhere the cocktail had landed. His reflexes were usually a bit better than that, but he hadn't moved in time to duck the unexpected assault. Too distracted by the cute waitress. The one who stood gaping at him, a slight smile of amusement quivering along her lips.

The perpetrator of the tequila toss had already made her way back to the refuge of her circle of friends. They each took turns throwing disgusted looks in his direction as the drink-flinger sniffled and wiped away a tear from her cheek.

For the life of him, he didn't recognize her. No doubt that was part of the problem.

The cute waitress was still there, clearly trying hard not to smile or laugh at him.

"Probably, huh?"

"Yeah. I'm usually a lot quicker to duck. She caught me off guard."

An elegant dark eyebrow arched up and she bit the inside of her cheek. Such an innocent gesture that somehow shot a surge of longing through his chest.

"Usually?" she asked. "Does this sort of thing happen to you often, then?"

"I'm going to opt not to answer that, if it's all the same to you." He smiled as he answered, then wiped a hand down his face to remove more of the moisture. "The ride home should be fun," he added.

She seemed to peruse him, her gaze traveling from his forehead down to his soaked shirt, then lower to his feet. She chewed her cheek some more, as if considering. Seemingly, she came to some kind of conclusion or decision.

"Here, follow me," she told him. Without waiting for any kind of answer, she turned on her heel and strode across the dance floor.

What choice did he have?

Gianni started after her, careful not to lose her in the throng of gyrating dancers.

He caught up to her at the bar where she took a left and headed toward a narrow hallway.

"Where are we going exactly?" he asked her back.

"There should be a dry shirt or two in the back office. Hopefully, one of them will fit."

They passed the restrooms and a utility door. Finally, she stopped at the last door and pulled a key ring out of her apron pocket. He followed her inside the room without any thought or hesitation. A strange and unexpected thought reared in the back of his mind—if this stranger asked him to, he'd follow her anywhere.

He gave his head a shake. Now he was just being fanciful. Sure, she was attractive. Hair so dark it was striking, olive skin, shapely in a way that screamed sultry. But she really wasn't his type. His type usually fell toward blonds with porcelain skin and yoga-toned physiques. A lot like the woman who'd just flung a drink at him, in fact.

"We always keep some clean clothes back here," she was saying. "For any bartenders or servers who might be having a clumsy night."

"Lucky for me."

She went into what looked like a utility closet and emerged holding a button-down short-sleeved cotton shirt with a band collar. Really not his style, though it wasn't as if he could be choosy at the moment. It would feel good to get the sticky wet shirt off once and for all.

"So, if you don't mind my asking, what brings you to the Carpe D?"

He had to chuckle at her question. He must have stuck out like a sore thumb out there.

"Why do you ask?" Rhetorical question. He knew the answer.

A small smile spread over her lips. "Let's just say you're not our usual niche of clientele. And I didn't see you on the dance floor even once."

He returned her smile. "Trust me, no one needs to see me dance."

"Then why?"

He shrugged, tried to choose his words carefully. Though he didn't want to lie to her, he couldn't exactly tell her the truth and risk the owner getting wind of his intention. Not just yet anyway.

"My brother's been talking up this place since it opened. He was supposed to come with me but something came up and he backed out." It was all completely true. Technically, he hadn't actually lied to her about anything. His *mamma*'s voice echoed through his head, telling him an omission of the truth was still a deceitful lie. But Mamma's strict code of ethics could be taken with a grain of salt given the reality he'd grown up with.

"Something came up, huh?" she asked.

"Yeah. Very last minute. So I figured I'd just check it out finally even though I'd be alone."

Her eyes narrowed on his. She looked suspicious. He diverted by changing the subject. "So, I didn't catch your name."

She gave her head a shake. "Sorry. Very rude of me. I'm Laney."

He nodded. "Laney. Pretty name. I'm Gianni Martino."

"Nice to meet you." She chewed her bottom lip. "Sorry your first time here is ending on such a sour note." She motioned to his wet chest. "If it makes you feel better, my evening didn't start out all that great either."

"Oh?"

She shook her head. "I was unceremoniously dumped. Over the phone, no less. He didn't even have the decency to come by and do it in person." Her gaze dropped to her feet. "He told me I bored him."

There was genuine hurt threaded through her tone. "He sounds like quite the fool."

She lifted her head back up.

He continued, "I know we just met, but that's the last word I would use to describe you."

"Oh? Why's that?"

"Everything from the way you're dressed to the way you make a living tells me you're far from dull. Tell me, what does this ex of yours do?"

"He's an accountant."

Of course. He had to laugh out loud at that. "Just as I guessed, clear case of projection if you ask me."

She tilted her head in question. "Come again?"

He shrugged. "Sounds like he's the one guilty of the accusations he's throwing around. The man probably figured he'd get out before you came to your senses and realized who the really boring one in the relationship is."

She tapped her chin with a perfectly manicured nail. "I see you might have a point. The man's idea of a good time is to play a round of golf, then sit in the clubhouse for several hours after." She looked up at him, blinking. "You're right! I'm not the boring one. He is. Thank you."

"You're welcome. Glad to be of service."

His reward was a wide smile. "Well, Gianni. Typical client or not, I'm glad you came in. Despite the minor scene out there."

She'd surprised him with her admission. "Me too. Drink attack and all."

"I hope you'll come back."

He had no doubt about it. "Definitely. I know I will."

"Glad to hear it."

A heavy moment of silence ensued. She seemed to have a rare magnetism that steadily pulled him toward her orbit. He'd never experienced anything like it before. Gianni grasped for something to say. He couldn't explain his strong reaction to her, not even to himself. An intense electricity seemed to be crackling between them. The term "sparks fly" came to mind. He'd never experienced anything so heady in the presence of a woman he'd just met.

Stop it already.

There he was being all imaginative again. He'd just met the woman for heaven's sake.

"You probably want to get out of that wet shirt."

Grabbing the hem of his pullover, he pulled it off over his head. He looked up to find her studying him, from his waistband over his stomach to his chest, then his shoulders. When her gaze returned to his, something had shifted in her eyes. They'd grown darker, heavy-lidded. She apparently liked what she saw.

He knew raw attraction when he saw it. If there'd been any doubt about the subtle pull between them earlier, there was no mistaking it now. And it was most definitely mutual.

Laney had no way of describing the wanton attraction that seemed to be humming over her skin straight through to her core. And she certainly couldn't explain why she'd confided in him, a mere stranger really, about her breakup. Yet, the way he'd tried to reassure her had sent a curl of warmth from her chest down to her belly. Maybe he had a point. Now that she thought about it, what exactly did Joseph think made him so exciting in comparison? He certainly couldn't hold a candle to the man standing before her now.

Even before he'd taken his shirt off and she'd laid eyes on that washboard stomach and finely chiseled chest. When had she ever gawked at a man before? But here she was now, her mouth not working, unable to tear her gaze away from his bare skin.

Finally, Gianni cleared his throat, pulling her out of her reverie. His gaze fell to the shirt she held in her hands, further jarring her into the present.

"Oh! I'm so sorry. Here you go," she blurted as she handed it to him. What a shameful reaction to a man simply taking his shirt off. She felt the sting of embarrassment heat up in her cheeks.

As he took it from her, their fingertips brushed ever so slightly. A lightning bolt of electricity seemed to shoot from her hand straight through to her very center. She let her arm linger, still touching his hand.

Snap out of it!

What was wrong with her? She was acting like a schoolgirl who'd just been approached by the high school quarterback in the hallway between classes.

Only, when she looked back up to the stranger's face, there was no mistaking the heat behind his eyes. Maybe it was merely wishful thinking on her part, but it appeared her attraction to this man wasn't exactly one-sided. He confirmed that suspicion when he took an ever so slight step in Laney's direction, and her breath suddenly grew heavier. What might happen if she took a step too? They'd be within a hair's width of each other, close enough to kiss.

Did she dare?

A sudden vibrating in her back pocket along with the sound of her ringtone yanked her out of the moment. She thought about ignoring it, but maybe the interruption had happened for a reason. The atmosphere had grown much too thick with tension.

"Excuse me." Reluctantly, she dropped her arm and reached for her cell phone.

The photo appearing on the screen was her sister's profile picture. What a way to be pulled back to reality.

Gianni gave her a nod, indicating she should go ahead and take the call. In one fluid motion, he pulled the shirt over his head to put it on. What a shame.

"Hey, Em. Can I call you back? I'm working." A fact her sister was very well aware of.

Not surprisingly, Emily didn't heed her request. "Okay. But, just real quick, have you and Joseph signed off on the hotel room?"

Laney swallowed. At some point, she was going to have to tell Emily and her parents that she'd be attending her sister's wedding events solo. Not something she was looking forward to. And definitely not something she was at all prepared to do just yet. Especially not with the tall dark and handsome stranger standing just a couple of feet away.

For one selfish moment, Laney wanted to pretend the call had dropped and hang up on her sister. To return her focus back to Mr. Chiseled Jaw. But it was too late; he was already turning away and heading back out the door. He mumbled something about making sure to return the borrowed shirt over his shoulder as he walked out.

An irrational sense of loss struck at the center of her chest. She had half a mind to call him back. To then say what? How pathetic it would sound to simply ask him to stay. She had no reason to do so. So she just watched as he shut the door behind him and released a heavy sigh. She shouldn't have expected anything to go her way today of all days.

Would she ever see him again? Why did she so badly want to?

"Are you even listening, Laney? Laney? Elaine!" Laney jumped, jarred by the use of her proper name. Her sister demanded an answer through her phone speaker.

"Everything's all set," she responded, lying to her sister because she simply couldn't get into the mess that was her personal life right now. "Don't worry about anything. Your wedding is going to go off without a hitch."

She could hear Emily's sigh of relief over the phone. "Thanks, sis. I know I'm approaching bridezilla level here. I just want everything to go smoothly."

"It's okay. I'll call you later, Em. I really do have to go," she said gently before clicking off the call.

Laney loved her sister, she really did. But Em could be a bit highly strung at times. And her approaching wedding had somehow severely exaggerated that trait. Not that anyone could fault Emily for her type-A personality. Look at how far it had gotten her in life. A steadily advancing career as a junior lawyer, countless accomplishments and awards within her industry, and now her engagement to a seemingly perfect all-American up-and-coming investment banker.

Yep, by all standards, her sister was the very embodiment of success. Everything her parents could have hoped for. Just like Mom and Dad, in fact. Wealthy, established, highly regarded in their field.

Unlike their other daughter.

In contrast to her sister, Laney had dropped out of school rather than go on to earn an advanced degree in law. After leaving school to pursue her dream of becoming a dancer, Laney had been rejected audition after audition. She'd decided to do the next best thing—find a way she could be near music and dancing while she made a living. So, instead of investing the nice nest egg that their grandfather had left them the way Emily had, Laney used hers to open a nightclub. While Emily had followed in their parent's pedigreed and polished footsteps, Laney had taken the road less traveled.

May they one day forgive her for it.

Somehow their differences were made all the worse because Laney was older by two years. But Emily was the one everyone had always admired and looked up to. Even Laney herself. Who could blame her? Unlike her, Em never felt out of place or like a square peg in a round hole.

And now Laney was going to have to go and explain to all of them yet another failure. She was certain she'd dodged a bullet. After all, if Joseph could be so cold and callous after two years of dating, sooner or later that defect in his character was going to emerge.

Still, on the surface Laney just knew it was going to look like she'd somehow managed to foul up yet another good thing she'd had going for her. No doubt, her parents would ultimately find a way to blame her. It would hardly matter that he'd almost certainly been cheating on her. Somehow, she'd be found to be the one to blame for his indiscretion.

Never mind that she was a successful businesswoman who owned a very popular nightclub. In her family of academic highbrow professionals, her chosen professional path was nothing to be impressed by in comparison.

Laney released another deep breath and plopped down in her office chair. No wonder she'd felt so attracted to a random stranger. She was looking for assurance that she was still attractive, that someone could still want her.

She had to admit she was feeling dejected. She really hadn't seen the breakup coming. That Joseph had told her she was boring just added jagged-edged rock salt into the open gaping wound.

It had started to feel awkward, with him just standing there getting dressed as she talked on the phone. If he were being completely honest with himself, he'd felt a little rattled at the way she affected him. So he made his escape. Some might call that cowardly. Or simple self-preservation. He was going to go with the latter.

It was bad enough she had no clue who he was or why he was there. And as he pulled up into the parking of the twenty-four-hour boxing gym, he still hadn't been able to put Laney out of his mind.

A nagging sensation tickled the back of his mind. During her phone call, the person on the other end had been loud enough that he'd heard part of the conversation. He could have sworn the caller had called Laney "Elaine."

Pulling out his smartphone, he called up his business drive and opened the file on acquisitions to confirm. And there it was in black-and-white on the small screen, just as he'd suspected.

Owner/proprietor of intended property: Elaine Taytum.

Elaine. Laney. A quick online search of various local business pages verified his conclusion. She wasn't a cocktail waitress at all. She was merely waitressing at her own establishment.

Gianni bit out a sharp curse. Way to complicate things even further given the fierce attraction he felt toward her as soon as they'd met.

All the better that he was here at the gym. A few rounds with a heavy punching bag would go far to settling some of the inexplicable frustration he was feeling.

Something about the woman had triggered a need in him he hadn't even realized he had. Less than ten minutes later, he was changed and pummeling the bag. Only two other men were also present, sparring in the center ring. Within no time, Gianni's heart rate was pumping and sweat rolled down his face.

Though it took a while, the exertion finally started to temper the storm of relentless angst he'd been feeling since he'd left the Carpe D.

"Thought I'd find you here," a familiar masculine voice bellowed behind him. "You're not answering your phone."

Gianni stopped mid punch and turned to face his brother. Angelo was the complete opposite of him in every way. Fair where Gianni was tan, not exactly short but nowhere near Gianni's six foot one. Angelo's amber-hued eyes changed color with the light, whereas Gianni's were perpetually dark. Angelo was a devoted family man. And Gianni would never follow that path, he was almost certain. Falling for someone meant opening yourself to humiliation and hurt. Hurt that could spread out toward others like ripples in a pond after a boulder fell into it. For two men who were brothers, the differences between them ran surface level as well as far deeper.

They both knew the reason for that—a poorly kept secret that no one dared to talk about.

Still, despite that damning secret and all their differences, they'd always been close as siblings. Gianni would trust his brother with his very life.

"Planned on calling you as soon as I was done," he told the other man, taking his gloves off and reaching for the towel at the nearby weight bench.

"Did you scope the place out?"

"I did. Even met the owner."

"And? Will it work? Dad's going to want a full account in the morning."

Taking a swig from his ice-cold water bottle, Gianni nodded. "It's perfect. The location, the building." He poured a small amount of the water over his head. "Popular place though. Must do well. I don't see her accepting just any offer."

He'd intentionally gone on a night he'd known would be busy, to stay as under the radar as possible. Just a regular guy out for a fun night of clubbing.

Angelo shrugged. "Then we'll just make her an offer she can't refuse, won't we?"

Something told him things wouldn't be that simple. From what little he'd seen of her tonight, Laney wasn't going to fold easy about any kind of deal. She was obviously hands-on, to get into the grind of serving as a waitress. And she cared enough about her clientele that she made sure one of them didn't go home in a soaking wet shirt. Efficient and prepared.

What kind of man would have dumped such a dynamic, successful, attractive woman? It made no sense where he was standing. He gave his head a shake. He couldn't go there again. He'd barely just managed to get inappropriate thoughts of her out his mind. "We're going to have to."

His brother clapped him on the shoulder. "Sorry I couldn't come with you. Had a pounding headache that's only just receding."

"Don't worry about it. Glad you're feeling better."

"Probably coming down with what Marie and the kids had last week."

Gianni stepped back in exaggeration and used

his fingers to make the sign of an *x*. "Stay back and keep your germs to yourself."

Angelo rolled his eyes. "Ha-ha. Really funny, bro."

"I'm not exactly sure if I'm really joking, man."

Angelo ignored him and continued, "So I'll see you at breakfast tomorrow at Mom and Pop's, right?"

Gianni couldn't resist the temptation to tease him just a bit more. "I was thinking of skipping that. Seeing as those loud and bratty toddlers of yours will be there."

The statement couldn't be further from the truth. Seeing Angelo and Marie's two-year-old son, Gino, and four-year-old daughter, Gemma, was the highlight of Gianni's week every Saturday. He loved being able to spoil them, then hand them right back when the visit was over.

Angelo gave him a fake glare. "More funniness. You know, if working for the family business doesn't pan out for you, you should go out on a comedy tour."

Now, that was the real joke. As if Gianni had any real choice in his place within the Martino empire of entertainment companies. His wasn't the type of family where one of only two sons could easily walk away from the family business. His father valued loyalty and family above all else. Particularly when it came to his older son. Their empire included everything from gaming halls, to small-scale casinos, to fitness centers and gyms. And Franco wanted Laney's location as the next Martino casino. "Maybe I will."

"You do that. In the meantime, you can give the old man a complete rundown of what you saw tonight when we see him at breakfast tomorrow."

Gianni figured he would leave out the part about having a cocktail thrown in his face. And all that transpired afterward with the club's owner. If his brother and father ever got wind of any of that, he'd no doubt never hear the end of it.

"Yeah, yeah. I'll be there," he answered and reached for his bag on the nearby weight bench.

He'd have to get his thoughts in order before the morning when his father would undoubtedly have numerous questions about how to proceed with the acquisition. He'd also have to explain to his brother and father that Laney was probably going to be a tougher negotiator than they'd assumed.

CHAPTER THREE

SHE'D GOTTEN ZERO SLEEP.

It didn't help that the bridesmaid's dress she'd laid out to steam the other day seemed to be mocking her from across the room. She was supposed to be wearing that dress while walking in the bridal procession on Joseph's arm.

How in the world was she supposed to break it to her sister that she'd be attending solo? Emily would have to find somebody to take Joseph's place in the wedding party. Wayne, her soon-to-be brother-in-law, was probably going to have to ask one of his friends to step up. He'd have to explain that Emily's boring sister had been dumped on the eve of her sibling's wedding.

Luckily, her sister had decided the groomsmen should be clad in black tie, which meant standard tuxes. At least they wouldn't have to worry about scheduling a new fitting for someone.

It was all so humiliating. Laney didn't consider herself a particularly prideful person. But this was a bit too much to bear.

Her ex's words echoed through her head. *I'm breaking up with you and your first response is to wonder how you're going to break the news to others.*

Did Joseph have a point? What did it say about her that rather than experiencing loss or sorrow about the end of her long-term relationship, she felt anger more than anything else?

Puffing out a frustrated sigh, she shifted to her side. There was no point in pondering any of it right now. She had things to do, decisions to make. Maybe she should just drop out of the wedding procession altogether. Let Em's best friend Lea take over the duties as maid of honor. That thought had tears stinging her eyes. Even if they weren't particularly close, Emily was still her only sibling.

No, she wasn't going to let a philandering ex mar her only sibling's wedding for her.

One thing was certain, as sleepless as she was, she was going to need a whole pot of coffee to get her through the morning. There was the exercise class to teach—Laney had gotten the idea a few months back that she could use the club dance floor for pop-up fitness classes, having been certified since college as an instructor. It didn't provide for a huge revenue stream, but it made more sense than to let the club just sit empty all day. With the added benefit that she got some exercise and met so many more people.

And she was still working on that cocktail recipe for tonight's house special. She couldn't continue to wallow in bed, no matter how groggy she felt.

With a resigned sigh, she threw her covers off and sat up. In between all she had to do, she would have to somehow rehearse exactly what she was going to say to Emily and her parents.

She could just imagine their distressed, yet somehow resigned, reactions. Here was Laney yet again disappointing everyone. Her parents kept expecting her to fail, and she kept proving them right.

They'd undoubtedly ask if Laney had tried hard enough to make things work, especially given the close proximity to the big event. They'd wonder if she'd been the one to somehow mess things up between her and Joseph. She'd finally found someone they could approve of and she couldn't hold on to him.

At least the recipe for the cocktail was fairly close. A combination of elderflower, sparkling water and orange liqueur, she knew she needed just one more ingredient to bind it all together.

Hopefully, it would be a hit and nobody would get splashed in the face with the concoction through the course of the evening, unlike last night. The scene from the previous evening came flooding back into her mind. Images of the tall dark stranger standing in her office as he took his shirt off. The electricity that seemed to hum between them.

What might have happened if Emily hadn't called when she did?

Perhaps they would have exchanged numbers, and she'd be spending this morning wondering if he would call her today or if he would call her at all.

Laney gave her head a brisk shake. She had to have been imagining the tension that seemed to have existed between them. No doubt her mind was grasping at random possibilities simply because she'd been dumped only hours before a handsome and *very* toned Adonis stood shirtless in her office. After all, if he'd really wanted to get in touch with her again, there were plenty of times he could have asked for her number up until Em's phone call. Or he could have simply hung around afterward. But when she'd walked back out to the club, he was nowhere to be found.

Laney couldn't deny the disappointment she'd felt. She'd never met anyone quite so…well, like him. It was the only description that came to mind. He clearly wasn't some kind of office desk jockey. If he was, the man must spend the rest of the hours of his day just working out. Maybe he was a fitness instructor himself only full time.

Maybe he was a male model. Boston did have several marketing agencies that did business throughout the whole world.

She chuckled out loud. The chances of an up-and-coming male model being interested in her would be considered slim to none. Those types wanted glamour and style. She was neither of those things. As she'd found out when she was rejected again and again from any kind of respected dance company.

What was she thinking, anyway? She'd literally just gotten out of a long relationship. She had no business pondering the prospect of starting another one. Joseph's betrayal was going to take time to heal from. She'd trusted him, only to have him drop her at the most inopportune time, when she needed him to be there for her. Not to mention the whole cheating thing. It would take a while to get past all that.

And the risk of falling for a disastrous rebound fling was all too real, especially given her reaction to Gianni at the club.

No, she had to accept the reality that she was single now and she had to get on with her life. And she had to forget about the dark and handsome stranger who had so briefly walked through it.

* * *

Having never gotten around to purchasing a washer and dryer for his own place after a relatively recent move, Gianni made sure to do his laundry at his parents' home every Saturday when he went there for breakfast. That's why he was in possession of a freshly washed borrowed shirt that one Laney Taytum had given him when he drove away from his family's house close to noon. He'd tossed it in a paper bag and thrown it on the passenger seat.

The sooner he returned the shirt, the sooner he could put the encounter with Laney out of his head. Maybe then he could finally start viewing her as the next businesswoman he'd be negotiating a deal with rather than the sexy server who'd knocked the wind out of him.

Given the conversation he'd just had at breakfast with Angelo and his father, there was no doubt Martino Entertainment Enterprises was on a direct course to obtain the property and building that housed the nightclub she owned. It was the ideal spot for the gaming hall slash casino they'd had in development for the past year. Laney's club was situated right off the water on a small peninsula that used to house a lighthouse.

He'd been charged with making it happen.

The Carpe D was certain to be closed this time of day. But he'd noticed a mail drop box mounted on the outside by the entrance when he'd been there last night, and it so happened the club wasn't that far out of his way.

A surprising number of cars sat in the parking lot when he arrived several minutes later. Which made no sense for a nightclub, seeing as it was barely lunchtime. Was she holding some kind of training for the staff?

As he got out of the car, the pounding pulse of bass from a hip-hop song he recognized thumped through the air. A female voice sounded over the loud music.

Curiosity piqued, he approached the entrance.

He'd been mistaken. The club was definitely not closed. About twenty women in spandex and sneakers were bouncing on the dance floor in tandem—along with one solitary gentleman who appeared to be holding his own. Then they all started doing some complicated side-step move, which took them all around the dance floor.

But Gianni's focus was centered on one woman and her alone. And the sight of her made his gut tighten with desire.

Laney stood in front of the group on a makeshift wooden stage about five-inches high. She wore a bright green tank top, which fit her like a glove and brought out the tan, golden hue of her skin. Her toned shapely legs kicked to the music as the others followed her lead.

She was instructing some sort of fitness class and damned if it wasn't the sexiest scene he'd ever laid eyes on.

He stood watching, mesmerized as she thrust her hips forward and back, then did a mini twirl. Gianni swallowed. Exercise classes like this one certainly didn't happen at the boxing gyms his family owned and he frequently visited. Good thing too, since their usual clientele would no doubt drool all over the equipment if they were to witness something like this in the center ring, just like Gianni was on the verge of doing.

He continued to watch as the group came to a stop and the music ended. The next song to come on was a much slower one. He could barely hear Laney's voice but it sounded like she was congratulating everyone on a job well done before starting a cooldown.

She bent down and touched her toes, perfectly bent at the waist. The woman was definitely flexible.

Steady, fella. She's simply exercising. Nothing to get worked up about.

Gianni made himself look away and glanced around him. Thank the spirits above that no one else was nearby as he looked suspiciously like a solitary male in a parking lot gawking at a bunch of ladies—and one man—in tight fitness gear, bouncing around a dance floor.

If he were smart, he'd make a break for it right now before anyone noticed him. The class was clearly about to end. He could always drop the shirt in the mail. He started to do just that, about to pivot on his heel and get back in the car, but he didn't manage to move fast enough. As soon as Laney straightened, her eyes found his through the glass door of the entrance.

She gave him a wide smile, one that seemed to spread through her whole face. He might even surmise that she was happy to see him. Then she lifted a finger in the universal sign that said, *Give me a minute.*

What choice did he have?

She wrapped up the class in under a minute while Gianni waited, leaning against the hood of his car. Now that he'd been spotted, he felt less like a sneaky voyeur and he allowed himself to fully indulge in the view of Laney going through the steps of her cooldown stretches. If he'd only known he'd be treated to such an entertaining scene when he woke up this morning, it definitely would have given him something to look forward to.

Finally, her muscle-strained students started to trickle out and Gianni made his way inside. Laney waved when he made it to where she stood on the stage.

"Hey there." She was breathless, her cheeks pink with a slight sheen of sweat over her skin.

"Hey. I wanted to return this. Didn't mean to distract you during class."

She took the package from him. "You didn't. We were just wrapping up when I saw you. Hope you didn't wait out there long."

He merely shook his head. She'd certainly been worth waiting for.

Pointing to the bag she held, he said, "It's laundered. Nice and clean and fresh."

"Thank you for doing that."

"Thank you for not letting me drive home sticky and wet."

"You're welcome." An awkward pause ensued where Gianni knew he should walk out and leave but he just didn't want to. He enjoyed this woman's company, chatting with her was easy and pleasurable. Laney finally broke the silence. "You should attend the class sometime," she told him. "You might even have fun."

He spread his hands out and shook his head with exaggeration. "No one needs to see me try to do any of that. I don't think my hips would even move that way."

She appeared to study him from head to toe. "Something tells me you're coordinated enough for a Zumba class."

"Probably for the best if we don't try to find out."

She laughed, lifted the bag. "You know you didn't have to come all the way out here just to drop this off. You could have just brought it next time you came to the club. Unless..."

She didn't need to say the rest. She'd deduced the truth pretty much. That he had no intention of coming back to the club after this. Not to just hang out, anyway. He didn't deny it now. Her lips turned downward once more.

There was no mistaking the disappointment that darkened her eyes.

Laney couldn't deny the surge of pleasure that she felt when she'd seen him waiting in the parking lot.

What effect did this man seem to have on her? Was it simply the need to feel some sort of validation after being so soundly, humiliatingly rejected by her ex-boyfriend?

Something told her it wasn't that simple. Whatever it was, she had to get over it. Clearly, it was one-sided. He'd practically just admitted he'd had no intention of stopping by the club. Which left no doubt that he had no plans to try to see her again in the future. This was simply a coincidence. He just happened to come by during her Saturday morning dance class.

His next words confirmed that fact. "So, this is quite the setup. I didn't realize you also did fitness classes."

She made sure to hide the sinking feeling in her chest. How silly of her to feel so disappointed that he only came upon her by chance. "It's just a side thing. I happen to be certified and have all this space."

"Some added revenue?"

She nodded. "It allows me to up the wages I pay my workers. Not by much but it's something."

"That's very decent of you."

Laney was about to reply that all her employees felt like family—some of them even more so than her true kin. Her employees didn't look at her with clear disappointment in their eyes the way her parents and sibling did. She wanted to ensure all her staff were well compensated for their hard work. But they were interrupted by the sound of the door opening. Laney knew who it was without having to look up. Louise Miller was a regular in her Saturday class and managed to leave something behind almost every time. Last week it was her reusable water bottle.

Sure enough, it was Louise who noisily entered. "I forgot to grab my mat," the blond ponytailed, frazzled mom announced as she ran to the spot she'd occupied for the last forty-five minutes. She usually carpooled to the class with four other women from her neighborhood. "Great class, by the way," Louise continued. "We really enjoyed the music, as usual."

Laney gave her a smile of thanks.

"And sorry none of us could stick around to taste test that drink," Louise added over her shoulder as she ran back out the door.

"It's okay, Louise. Have a good week," Laney answered.

Gianni was giving her a quizzical look when she turned back to him. "You also do drink tastings?"

"Not regularly. I'm working on a new special cocktail for tonight. Just wanted some feedback but no one could stay this week."

A dark eyebrow lifted. "Maybe I can be of help."

"Oh?"

"I happen to be a great taste-tester." He added with a charming smile, "And I do like cocktails."

Well, that was unexpected. "Is that so?"

"Yep. As long as I don't down a full one. Then I'd have to call a car service. But I'd be happy to step in as your official taster."

"You would?"

"Sure. Sounds fun."

"That's great. You definitely don't have to drink a full one. And I can brew you a whole pot of coffee after."

"Sounds like a deal," he said with that breathtaking smile.

Suddenly, her afternoon was looking much more entertaining than the original one she'd planned for, pouring and stirring alone in her bar. She tried to clamp down on her excitement when she answered, "Then give me just a second to freshen up in the back. I'll meet you at the bar in just a few minutes."

He winked at her, just as he had last night, and her knees grew a little weak. It had nothing to do with the repetitive squats she'd been doing earlier during the "legs" portion of her class either. "Don't take too long. I'm pretty thirsty."

Made sense. She got the gut feeling that Gianni was the type of man who wasn't kept waiting too often. Particularly not by members of the opposite sex.

"I'll be there in no time," she assured him. "Just have to make myself somewhat presentable."

"I think you look great."

Was he flirting with her? Or did oozing charm just come naturally to someone like him?

Probably a little of both, no doubt.

Whatever it was, she felt a surge of giddiness rush through her at his compliment. When was the last time someone, a man in particular, had actually paid her any kind of praise?

Joseph was always, oh, so quick with the digs. Her hair was too messy, her dress too short. Her nails were the wrong color if she so much as tried anything bolder than plain beige or clear polish.

To think, he had the nerve to accuse *her* of being boring.

But his compliments had been few and far between. Since her breakup, Laney was beginning to see just how emotionally lacking her past relationship had been.

A parting glance at the man before her as she walked away only served to affirm that thought. As she freshened up in the ladies' room, a far-flung idea began to form in her head. He really was very handsome. And full of personality and humor. The kind of man any woman would be excited and thrilled to be with.

The perfect date to bring to a wedding.

She stared at her reflection in the mirror and gave her head a shake. *Nah*. How would she even begin to ask him something like that? But what was the alternative? She didn't have any really close male friends. And as luck would have it, all her close female friends wouldn't be able to help either. Rachel and Leigh were both only children. Carla had two sisters and Miranda's brother was overseas on active duty. Laney's only alternative was to fess up to her family.

Plus…the idea wasn't without appeal. For one thing, she'd get a chance to see him again. She would have to run it by her sister, of course. But Emily would be agreeable to the idea, Laney was certain. Her sister didn't want the snafu of a missing groomsmen this close to the big day. Still, as far as ideas went, it was loony and hare-brained and impulsive.

But it just might work.

CHAPTER FOUR

WHEN LANEY RETURNED about ten minutes later, she'd donned a long-sleeved hoodie and gathered her hair into a neater bun. Her cheeks were still slightly pink, but her face had been scrubbed clean.

She looked downright fetching. For an insane moment, he thought about what it might feel like to unzip the hoodie and remove the spandex underneath.

Don't even think it.

What was wrong with him?

The now-familiar hint of guilt fluttered in his chest once more. He really couldn't say why he'd offered to stay and help her play mixologist. But the way she'd told him about making sure to take care of her employees had tugged at him. How very intriguing that she was so worried about those she employed. He simply wanted to know more about her and what made her tick. It certainly couldn't hurt to learn more about her before offering a deal. He'd simply be doing research, so to speak.

He was going to have to find a way to come clean to her. Somehow. And soon. Plus, he'd have to reassure her that said employees would be taken care of once Martino Entertainment Enterprises bought her out.

But first things first.

"So, I can't decide if it should be vodka-based or gin," she was saying now and pulling out several bottles, which she placed on the bar between them. She then grabbed a cocktail tumbler and a small shot glass.

"The other ingredients are elderberry syrup and orange liqueur. Plus, I think it needs something else. I just can't seem to come up with what."

"Wow. Sounds flavorful." He looked on, intrigued as she poured very small amounts of each into the shot glass, then slid it to him across the bar.

He took a small sip. It was good. Really good. But she was right, it did need something else. Something subtle. "Basil," he said, as contrary as it sounded. But he knew he was right.

To her credit, she didn't argue the suggestion but quirked one elegant eyebrow. "Really? An herb?"

He nodded. "Trust me."

With a shrug, she turned her back and pulled

open a drawer. She returned with a basil leaf that she pinched between her thumb and forefinger before dropping it into the glass. He tasted it and his instincts were overwhelmingly confirmed.

"Not to pat myself on the back or anything, but it's right on the money." Without thinking, he handed her the glass. She took it and sipped with zero hesitation. Something about watching her drink from the same glass had his muscles tightening throughout his whole body.

Her eyes widened as she swirled the liquid around in her mouth. "It's fantastic! I would have never guessed."

He took a mock bow.

"But how? What made you think of basil of all things?"

"My *mamma* taught me to cook as soon as I could turn the oven on. It's all about intermingling various flavors. I don't see why a drink would be any different."

"Huh." She eyed him with appreciation clear in her gaze. He'd be lying if he said he didn't bask in it to a degree; he almost wanted to pound his chest like some kind of Neanderthal.

"You appear to be a man of many talents, Mr. Martino."

"You don't seem to be a slouch in the achievement department either, Miss Taytum."

Her eyes drifted downward, the smile on her

face flattened. Somehow the fun, lightheartedness of the moment seemed to dissipate in an instant.

"Was it something I said?" he asked. Though for the life of him he couldn't guess what it might have been. He'd just paid her a compliment, after all.

She seemed hesitant to answer. Finally, she looked up and the expression on her face reminded him of a wounded doe. "Let's just say that not many people feel that. That I'd be considered a success. And their thoughts on the matter will be once more affirmed next week at my sister's wedding."

None of that made any sense from where he was sitting. "How could that be? You're the owner of a very popular nightclub. And you're what? Twenty-eight? Twenty-nine?"

"Twenty-seven."

"So explain."

She shrugged. "It's all relative, isn't it? Whereas I dropped out of college, my father is a partner at a major Boston law firm, my sister is a junior associate at that same firm and my mom is a professor at New England Law."

He was beginning to see where she was coming from. Laney, for all her achievements, didn't seem to fit into the peg of her academically-oriented highbrow family. "Sounds like you just chose a different path. Nothing wrong with that."

"I guess." Her gaze darkened some more. "And now I have to find a way to tell them about my latest failure—my last relationship is a bust and that fact will throw off my sister's wedding. He and I were supposed to be a coupled part of the wedding party."

She gave her head a brief shake, handed him a bottle of water, then grabbed one for herself and took a long swallow. "But you don't need to hear about my family woes. Sorry to have gone on like that."

If she only knew. When it came to family dynamics, she wasn't the only one in the room with baggage. It surprised him how tempted he was to confide in her, to reveal his family's well-guarded secret to this woman he'd met just the night before. He'd never even considered sharing it with anyone before. He didn't even openly discuss the truth with Angelo, even though his brother had dropped hints over the years that he knew the truth as well as anyone. The truth being that Gianni wasn't actually Franco's son. That he was the product of an extramarital affair neither of his parents would acknowledge ever happened for their purely selfish reasons.

Not the time.

"No need to apologize," he said instead, seeking to reassure her. "I'm sorry to hear you're dealing with all that. Your ex left you in a pretty bad spot, didn't he?"

Her lips tightened. "He really did. With no regret whatsoever." She proceeded to call said ex several choice words, which would have impressed Gianni's buddies back at the gym.

"There's no one else who can step in?" he asked, thinking of a few choice words himself for the man who had put her in such an untenable position. He had to have known the rather tenuous relationship she had with her family and hadn't cared that he was exasperating it.

"I've been racking my brain and can't come up with anyone." Her eyes narrowed on him. "Unless…" She gave a nervous chuckle. "I don't suppose you're doing anything on the seventeenth? Just for the weekend?"

Huh. He hadn't seen that coming. The look of hope in her eyes hit him like an arrow to his chest. He knew he should say no. Things between them were complicated enough as it was. The attraction he felt for her was not easy to ignore. Given the reason he'd even met her in the first place, ignoring it was exactly what he should be doing. Not that she had any clue about any of that.

Which was the whole problem in and of itself.

Then again, maybe this would be an opportunity. A chance for them to get better acquainted before the deal making began. Nothing said the buyout had to be hostile. They might even be able to work out terms toward some kind of partnership.

Laney clapped her hand to her cheek, her mouth agape. "Oh, my! I really shouldn't have asked. What an awful position to put you in. I'm sorry. Please forget I even mentioned it."

He stood up from the bar stool and pulled his smartphone out of his back pocket and clicked the first icon. "You know what? According to my calendar, I am completely free that weekend. And it's been a while since I've been to a wedding."

Though she thought she'd been prepared for it, Laney still felt the rush of surprise at Gianni's answer. Deep down, she'd really doubted that he would say yes.

"Wait. Really? Are you really saying you'll come with me?"

He bowed slightly over the bar. "I'd be honored to accompany a lovely lady to her sister's wedding."

The relief she felt, straight to her core, was nearly palpable.

"Just one question. Won't they feel resentful later?" he asked. "When someone they don't really know is going to be part of this monumental day? Part of the photo albums? And all of that."

Of course, she'd thought of that. But given

the circumstances, it was something of a moot point. "That's going to be the case regardless of who steps in at this point. Everyone of import in Emily's life or Wayne's is already a part of the wedding party. And look how nonpermanent Joseph turned out to be." He seemed to mull over what she'd said.

"That would be the ex, I take it."

"You would be correct. Plus, I'd ask you to do one more thing, if you're comfortable." She was biting the corner of her cheek nervously again, but she couldn't seem to help it.

"What's that?"

"Could we pretend that we…you know…are kind of in a serious relationship? That it came fast and heavy and we were both taken by surprise? I know it's rather deceiving—"

He cut her off. "Say no more. I find nothing wrong with a little playacting given what's at stake. I'm glad I can be of help."

She released a deep sigh. "I don't know what to say. Aside from thank you. You have no idea how much this means to me." She held up her hands, palms up, hoping that he really understood where all this was coming from. "I hate that I'd be misleading my family, but I think this really would be best for everyone involved. At least until I can explain to them at a better time."

"I get it." He really seemed to. It sent a feeling of warmth and appreciation through her middle.

"You do?"

"Sure. Sometimes being part of a family is letting them believe what they want to believe—untruths they're vested in despite all evidence."

He sounded very sincere. Like he really did understand. Better than she could have guessed.

"You'd be surprised," he told her, as if reading her thoughts.

She waited for him to continue, didn't push when he failed to elaborate further. He changed the subject. "So, first things first, what's the venue? I'm guessing this is a formal affair. I already own a couple of tuxes."

"Yes. We'll need to get into all of that. Plus, I don't know all that much about you. Well, I know nothing about you, in fact."

"Nor I you. That is indeed a problem. We'll need to set aside some time and get into all of the unknowns. How about dinner tonight?"

"I can do that," she answered, then chuckled with a slow shake of her head.

"What?"

"I just can't believe that we're going through with this. That you've actually agreed to go along with it."

She could only hope they both knew what they were getting into.

CHAPTER FIVE

SHE COULD HAVE stumbled into a worse scenario than the one she was about to embark upon. Somehow, through some very random events, beginning with a tossed drink, Laney found herself about to dine with a gentleman she'd barely just met who was preparing a home-cooked meal for her so they could go over how to act like a committed couple. Gianni told her he wanted to show off his culinary skills, so he'd invited her to his apartment for what he called a *made-from-scratch, authentic-Italian meal*.

The thought of it made her mouth water as she walked up the steps to his brownstone. He lived just outside Boston's North End district, an area most other cities would call Little Italy. Even from this distance, the myriad of scents from the nearby restaurants, bakeries and grocery shops hovered in the air and further spurred her appetite.

Not to mention, the aroma coming from Gianni's apartment was just as enticing. She deeply inhaled it all as she pressed his doorbell. He answered within seconds. He wore a waist apron with a cartoon map of Italy. The T-shirt he had on wasn't exactly tight but fit him well enough to accent all those toned muscles of his chest and upper arms.

How did the man manage to look so gosh darn sexy wearing a cartoon apron for heaven's sake?

"Right on time," he said with that devilish smile she was starting to find so familiar and charming. "Welcome. Come on in."

He stepped aside, opening the door farther. That mouth-watering scent she'd been enjoying outside intensified, a heady mix of spices, garlic and tomato.

"I happen to be running a bit late," he informed her. "Dinner is still in progress."

"You didn't have to go through the trouble of cooking for me, you know," she told him. "But I definitely appreciate it. It smells delicious in here."

"I enjoy cooking, happy to do it."

She reached inside her oversized bag to pull out the host gift she'd brought. Gianni had told her he had the whole dinner planned and would take care of everything from the wine to the dessert. And she certainly didn't want to second-guess an expert Italian cook about any part of an Italian dinner. So she'd brought the only thing she could think of.

His smile grew as he took it from her. "A basil plant. Perfect." He gently pulled off a couple of the leaves. "I'll put this to use right now on the bruschetta."

She followed him down the hallway, farther into the apartment. He had some kind of hard rock track playing in the background, just loud enough to notice but not enough to recognize the tune.

"Is that what smells so divine?" she asked.

"That, plus the tomato sauce is simmering on the stove top."

He really knew what he was doing. "Can I help in any way?"

"Sure. Have you ever rolled gnocchi?"

She shook her head. "Can't say that I have. My culinary skills are limited to throwing some kind of meat in the oven and pressing start on the rice cooker."

He pointed behind him. "Then go wash up and get prepared for a brief lesson on gnocchi rolling. Washroom's through that door."

She did as instructed, and when she returned, Gianni handed her an apron of her own. A full-length one for her. "Don't want you staining that dress," he told her. "That would be a shame." His eyes traveled down the length of her body as he said it and she felt heat spread from her middle clear up to her face. It had nothing to do with the steam coming from the various pots on the stove.

Without responding to his comment, she pulled the apron over her head and tied the straps behind her back at the waist. She took her time in order to try to regain some of her composure after the effect of his words and gaze. She stepped over to the counter. "What can I do to help?"

Several thin rows of some kind of dough sat on the counter, fluffy white flour was sprinkled along the entire surface. Gianni took a large knife and deftly sliced each row into small pieces. He then grabbed a small wooden board with a handle and ridges on one side. "Here," he gently took her by the shoulders as he handed her the board. "Take a piece of the dough, and just sort of roll it down the board. But stop before the dough completely rolls on itself. You need a small gap in the middle."

She started to do as instructed, trying to focus fully on the task at hand. It wasn't easy with him standing so close. He reached inside the drawer for another board to use himself. Her first roll didn't turn out so great. Why was it so hard to concentrate on a simple task merely because he was near?

"You look confused," he said with an amused smile.

"Well, not to sound too uninformed, as I did admit my limited culinary talents earlier after all, but this seems like a lot of work. Can't we just cook the dough as these small pieces?"

He slowly shook his head. "I can't believe what I'm hearing. You need these ridges and the small opening in the middle so that the sauce can get into each nook."

She supposed that made sense. But understanding the concept wasn't exactly helping her with the process. All her pieces looked like mangled small pebbles.

Gianni must have taken pity on her. "Here, let me show you."

He stepped behind her and she lost her breath for a moment. Whatever aftershave he was wearing reminded her of nighttime walks along the beach. The heat from his body behind her seeped through her clothes to her skin. She could feel his warm breath on the back of her neck. Then he took her right hand in his own and proceeded to demonstrate exactly how to roll the small piece of dough down the board in one quick motion.

"See, easy as pie," he said against her cheek. "You think you've got the hang of it?"

Think? Who could think? As if Laney could even register anything but the feel of him against her back.

She nodded lamely and allowed him to continue guiding her.

"You're a natural," he declared.

A shudder ran through her as heat flamed over her skin. His breath was hot on her cheek. It would be so easy to turn her head back just enough to bring her lips closer to his. Would he kiss her? Or would he wait for her to make the first move? Heaven help her, she very likely would. Several beats passed with neither one moving so much as a muscle. The very air around them seemed to grow thick. Her pulse pounded in her ears and she couldn't seem to make her mouth work.

This was wrong. They barely knew each other. She'd just broken up with her boyfriend.

She had to pump the brakes.

As if sensing her thoughts, Gianni released a sigh behind her and it was enough to break the heated moment. Finally, he stepped back. Part of her felt relief. And another much more bothersome part of her felt sheer, stark disappointment.

One thing was certain. When Gianni Martino accompanied her to the wedding as her newest fling, she was going to have absolutely zero trouble pretending to be attracted to him.

He didn't even want to pretend anymore. Not to himself, anyway. He absolutely couldn't deny just how much he was attracted to this woman. Which really was rather inconvenient.

For a moment back there, before he'd regained

his senses, he'd come perilously close to reaching for her, then pulling her into his arms. From there, heaven only knew what might have happened. He imagined lifting her up, sitting her on the counter, then pulling her up against him as he finally indulged in the kiss he'd so often fantasized about.

Luckily, he'd somehow managed to resist.

The growing attraction between them was only going to further muddy an already rather complicated situation. He had nobody but himself to blame. Not that there was much he could do about it now. He couldn't very well renege on his commitment to attend her sister's wedding.

He should have never agreed to that. She'd just looked so forlorn and so down when she'd spoken about her family and all the ways she felt out of place within her own clan.

It had all tugged at his heart. They had more in common than she'd ever guess. It still felt a bit unsettling, how close he'd come to telling her about his own situation, as the unwanted and unplanned son of a father who only claimed him to save face. So that he could pretend his wife had never cheated.

Laney didn't need to know any of that about him or his family. What had made him come so close to telling her? He had to wonder if agreeing to go with her wasn't going to end up being a colossal mistake.

Speaking of mistakes—what had he been thinking, stepping behind her and holding her that way? The electricity between them right now practically crackled in the air.

"Am I doing it right? They look better, don't they?" she asked next to him now, finally breaking the loaded moment. She held up the latest gnocchi she'd just rolled.

He pretended to examine it closely. "It's a work of art. My *mamma* would be impressed."

"Ha! Somehow I doubt that."

But chances were she'd never even meet his *mamma*. He was only meeting her family due to a fluky set of circumstances neither one of them could have guessed before they'd laid eyes on each other.

He would have to tell her the truth as soon as their playacting was over. Right after the wedding. He would have to confess that it hadn't been mere happenstance that had brought him into her club that night.

Her reaction was probably going to be far from pleasant. But he would have to cross that bridge when he came to it. By then, he'd be able to prove himself to be someone she could trust, and she'd hopefully see that his heart had been in the right place even if he couldn't tell her.

And if she didn't?

Well, he wasn't going to allow himself to entertain that unpleasant possibility just yet. And he certainly wasn't going to let it spoil what was so far turning out to be a thoroughly enjoyable evening.

After all, what exactly was he supposed to tell her? That he also happened to be the black sheep of the family? But his similar status came about for an entirely different reason. A reason everyone in his orbit had denied and ignored his whole life. He'd only discovered said reason himself thanks to an aging uncle with loose lips when he'd visited Italy as a preteen.

He shook off the useless thoughts and made himself focus on the present. Laney stood staring at him, as if she'd noticed he'd drifted somewhere far away. He hadn't even noticed all the gnocchi was rolled already.

He gently took her by the shoulders and led her to one of the bar stools at the counter. "Enough work on your part. I'm dangerously close to being a bad host here. Have a seat while I finish up." He grabbed the bottle chilling in the ice bucket and poured her a glass of wine.

"If you're sure."

"Absolutely." He pointed to her midsection. "Take off that apron and assume honored-guest mode starting this instant."

She laughed and gave him a mock salute. "As you command, sir."

Within minutes, he had them both plated with the hot steaming entrée, bowls of crispy salad and perfectly toasted garlic bread. He'd done good, if he did say so himself. Laney looked impressed. Her next words confirmed it.

"My mouth is watering. You have outdone my wildest expectations."

He couldn't begin to deny the surge of pleasure at her compliment. It grew stronger when she took a bit of the food and groaned in pleasure. Every ounce of will he possessed needed to be summoned in order to avoid responding to that groan.

"Mmm. This is divine. Overwhelmingly good. Seriously, I would have been happy with a deli sandwich and some chips."

"You wound me with your low expectations of my talents."

She tilted her head and raised her wine goblet. "You're right. I admit to underestimating you. My deepest apologies."

Gianni tapped his glass to hers. "Apology accepted. So, tell me, what made you open up a dance club in Boston? Not a very typical career choice."

She chewed some more and swallowed. "It wasn't my first choice."

"No?"

Shaking her head, she set her fork down. "I left school to become a professional dancer."

She was certainly full of surprises. "You did?"

"Yep. Didn't exactly work out."

Gianni felt himself leaning closer to her over the table. "How so?"

"I tried out and auditioned for numerous companies and acts. Not a one bit." She gave a wistful shrug before continuing. "Just didn't have what it took, I kept being told."

He wanted desperately to go to her, take her in his arms and reassure her that she was more than enough as far as he could see. But he couldn't allow himself to do that. Besides, right now it sounded like a simple ear to listen was all she might need.

"So I came back to Boston with my tail tucked between my legs. After having let everyone down with my decision to *throw away* my future, as my mother and father put it."

"But you didn't go back to school."

She took another sip of her wine. "It's not for me. I'm not exactly the studious type. And I'm definitely not the type to sit in an office cubicle making phone calls or crunching numbers."

"So what happened?"

"As luck would have it, my reclusive grandfather left us a small sum of an inheritance. My sister invested her share in the market. And I invested mine in a different direction than the one I'd originally set for myself."

He was fascinated by her. Despite consistent disappointment, she'd somehow managed to find an alternate dream to pursue, then made it come true. "That's remarkable. Consider me impressed."

Gentle laughter escaped her lips. "Impressed? Did you hear the part about my numerous rejections as a professional dancer?"

"Yes. I also heard the much more important part."

Her gaze drifted downward before she cleared her throat, then changed the subject. "So what about you? Tell me about what you do."

His story wasn't nearly as interesting, but he began to tell her. "I work for an entertainment company. We own and run everything from gaming centers to small casinos, and a few gyms."

She raised an elegant eyebrow. "That sounds like quite an empire. What's your role?"

"I'm a VP in the office of the CEO. Who happens to be my father. He's a self-made businessman who started out small with a few gaming halls, which then led to small casinos and other entertainment venues. More recently, we've expanded into the fitness and gym arenas after I discovered kickboxing."

To his surprise, Laney seemed genuinely interested in the kickboxing piece. He explained his training routine and the various positions, both offensive and defensive. Before he knew it, they were halfway through with dinner.

There was no more delaying the inevitable. Laney apparently came to the same conclusion based on her next comment. "So I suppose we should start to talk about your newly acquired status as my significant other. And exactly what scenario we're going to present to the outside world next week."

She was right of course. But he couldn't help the small twinge of disappointment at the clear acknowledgment that this wasn't any kind of real date.

"I suppose you're right."

She turned in the stool to fully face him, all business suddenly. "We may as well start with the basics. How did we meet? I say we stick as close to the truth as possible."

The sincerity in her tone made it clear just how serious she was about all this going smoothly. How much it meant to her that her family believe she'd found a real and solid relationship after her last one had crumbled.

He could only hope he wouldn't let her down.

CHAPTER SIX

Two weeks later

HERE IT WAS—their first big test. Emily's wedding weekend. And it all started with a merry bash the night before the big day aboard a yacht for a sunset sail. The entire wedding party and a few distinguished guests were being treated to a three-hour cruise along Boston harbor. Gianni had picked her up so that they could drive in together. Laney tried to swallow down the queasy feeling in her throat as Gianni pulled his late-model sports car into the underground parking lot of the hotel that was to house the festivities for the next couple of days.

Between all the last-minute wedding details and her sister's and parents' work schedules, they'd never actually met Gianni. So tonight was going to be all or nothing as far as impressions went. They'd reacted just as she'd expected when she told them about Joseph's sudden rejection. Hence, she'd spared Gianni no amount of praise and compliments as she described him to her family, somewhat softening the blow from the announcement of her breakup.

She glanced at him now as he killed the ignition and gathered his wallet from the dashboard. He was everything a girl would want to bring home to the folks. Handsome, successful, personality in spades. And he could cook! A soft flush of heat warmed her cheeks as she thought about that night two weeks ago in his apartment when he'd stood up so close to her, the scent of him tempting all her senses. The same scent which filled the car right now. That night had been the last time they'd been physically together to try to hash out the plan. Only a handful of phone calls had taken place between them since. Their work schedules just hadn't seemed to mesh.

A curtain of panic dropped over her. Sweet heavens. What if they hadn't thought of and prepared for all the ways this harebrained plan could go, oh, so wrong.

"You ready for this, sweetheart?" he asked.

Laney pressed her hand to her middle to quell the sudden nervous nausea. "Not sure that's the right question."

"No?"

"A better question might be if my family is ready and willing to accept what we're about to try to pull off."

He gave her a warm smile that she was sure was meant to comfort. "Hmm. How about we just look at it as more like simply attending a party together?"

As if she could ignore the true reality of what tonight and tomorrow were really about. "Sure. Let's go with that."

He winked at her. "That's the spirit."

At least one of them had their wits about them. Though Gianni had so much less to lose if everything went south.

Without giving her any warning, he gently took her hand in his and leaned toward her in the passenger seat. "Hey, relax. Everything will run smoothly. We'll be convincing as the budding, infatuated couple we're meant to play."

A voice in her head taunted that one of them would be playacting just a bit more than the other. But that was neither here nor there. Right now, they had a party cruise to get ready for.

"Right. Let's get up to the room, then. I could use time to freshen up a bit and change into my dress."

"You got it."

Before she could so much as unbuckle her seat belt, he was outside her door and opening it for her, then he helped her out and even grabbed her two carry bags.

"I'll let you grab the garment bag with the

dress," he said, shifting the seat to give her access to where it hung. "Don't want to be responsible for any wrinkles."

Beyond thoughtful and considerate. Laney had to bite back her longing. Why couldn't this be her reality? Why couldn't Gianni have been the man she'd spent the last two years with in a committed and rewarding relationship?

She could guess at the answer. She wasn't the type to really attract a man like him. Not beyond a surface chemistry. She'd found that out the hard way during her days in New York, then Los Angeles. And again, more recently with Joseph. She had more than her fair share of feeling unwanted for one lifetime.

Gianni was well rounded, smart, successful. And he even had something of an edge. He'd told her that night at dinner that his fitness routine was mainly kickboxing. Mostly with a bag out of the ring. Though he admitted to occasionally sparring with a partner *inside the ropes*, as he explained it. He even went so much as to compete in events sporadically.

Not exactly a noncontact sport. No, he was unlike her in every way, the polar opposite of boring.

She had to snap out of it. This was no time to wallow in self-pity. She was supposed to be half of a newly minted, infatuated couple. She had to look and act the part.

By the time they made it to the garage elevator, she'd managed to convince herself that she could do it without arousing any suspicion. Yes, they really could pull this off, her and Gianni. She just had to relax.

Besides, everyone would be much too focused on the bride and groom to take much notice of her and her new boyfriend. Including the bride and groom themselves.

She was fine. She just had to breathe. It was simply a matter of staying calm, she told herself.

Until she realized she was still clutching Gianni's hand in a viselike grip since he'd helped her out of the car several moments ago.

To his credit, he wasn't attempting to pull it away. Still, they weren't in the company of the others just yet. She had to save such images for when they'd be witnessed. Hesitantly, she pulled her hand away and pressed the button for the ground floor of the hotel.

Turning to Gianni, she cleared her throat. There was one small piece of the puzzle she hadn't wanted to get into, had procrastinated bringing it up until this very moment, in fact. "There's also something else you might want to be prepared for. About my parents."

He simply lifted a dark eyebrow.

"They might be a bit..." She faltered, searching for just the right words. She'd known this was going to be hard, and she hadn't been mistaken. "Let's just say, they're not the warmest, most affable people upon first meeting someone. I'm sorry, I should have mentioned that before."

"Don't worry, *cara*," he told her with another devastating smile. And she was just going to have to ignore the endearment or she might turn into a puddle on the floor. "I think I can handle them."

Laney only wished she could say the same.

She was downright terrified. Gianni wanted badly to simply pull her into his arms and rub out some of the tension stiffening her shoulders.

As far as her parents, Laney seemed to think she was announcing some surprising bit of information. Truth was, he'd long ago surmised her parents as much the way she'd just described. Everything she'd said about them so far gave every indication that they were probably distant and unapproachable.

So unlike Laney herself.

But like he'd just reassured her, he was certain he could hold his own with two staunch and serious professionals who would no doubt decide to dislike him on sight.

Not that it would be easy. Coming from a loud

and boisterous family of Italian heritage, he was used to being the recipient of big bear hugs and physical displays of affection and love from everyone—from toddlers to the elderly to frail *zias* and *nonnas* making their feelings well-known whether anyone was actually listening or not.

Gianni stepped aside once they got to the ground floor and Laney began their check-in as part of the wedding party. He found himself watching her as he so often did. Even dressed in leggings and an oversized T-shirt, she managed to appear graceful, elegant. Full of class.

Not exactly how he'd describe himself.

No. He had no illusions about any of it. For all intents and purposes, he was about to enter an alien and unfamiliar world. One where he'd be suppressing a good portion of his personality. While most of these people probably spent their off time in a book or on the golf course, his hobby of choice involved throwing punches in a boxing ring.

A crowd such as the one attending this wedding was sure to look down on such an unrefined, brutal activity. Not many people understood that it was a sport just like any other. One that focused on athleticism and discipline no less than other physical pursuits. He'd be willing to wager that he didn't get bruised and cut up any more than most other non-pro athletes. But he wasn't here to argue about the merits of his workouts. He was simply here to support Laney and in the process gain some of her trust.

The thought took him aback a bit. When he phrased it that way, it sounded conniving and wrong. But that wasn't his intention, to deceive her in any way. He just wanted them to be on better terms when he finally approached her with his family's offer to buy out her building and business.

"We're all set," she said, approaching him now and holding out a key card for the room.

"Thanks."

"Room 709. Supposed to be a great view of the harbor."

He had no doubt it would, along with everything else the Boston Harbor Hotel had to offer. Tourists and businesspeople from all over the world used this luxury hotel as their destination point when traveling to the area. Hardly a surprise that Laney's sister would be holding her wedding here.

Gianni wasn't exactly in the pauper category. In fact, his family was one of great wealth. His father owned gaming halls, fitness centers and casinos all over the world. But Papà had come from nothing—born in a poor remote village in the northern hills of Italy—and he'd fought and scrambled for all the material wealth he possessed. It was very obvious that Laney came from good old-fashioned American money. An entirely different category.

They were in their suite within a couple of minutes, the elevator ride spent mostly in silence. Gianni wracked his brain to come up with something to say that might lessen the tension that was emanating off her like a steady hum.

Then her gaze fell on the furniture in the room and he could practically feel her discomfort skyrocket. Rather than the full-sized couch they'd both assumed would be part of their furnishings—the couch Gianni had planned on sleeping on overnight—the master area of the suite consisted of two small love seats with a center wooden coffee table. He couldn't even help the images that sprung into his mind. The two of them together in the only bed, tangled up in the sheets and in each other. He shook his head to clear it.

"It's okay, Laney. I can sleep on one of those sofas."

She rolled her eyes. "You'd have to sleep sitting up."

"So be it."

"I wouldn't be able to sleep myself, knowing you were out here so uncomfortable."

"Then I'll just drive home if I have to."

She threw her hands up. "That's not any better. How am I supposed to feel knowing you were driving in the middle of the night after partying on board a boat?"

She really was wrapping herself up in figurative knots here. "Then I'll stay. I've slept in worse."

She shook her head. "I hardly think so."

He laughed, trying to reassure her. "You'd be surprised. Go take your shower. It might help relax you a bit."

"I doubt that," she argued.

It was worth a shot.

"Come on, Gianni," she continued. "We can't exactly pretend this isn't a very awkward set of circumstances."

He responded with a shrug. "It doesn't have to be."

As she chewed her bottom lip, it was clear she wasn't exactly convinced of his comment. She glanced at the digital clock hung on the wall by the large flat-screen television. "Well, I guess we'll have to figure it out at some point. The cruise takes off in a couple of hours. I'm going to take my shower. I won't be long."

"Take your time."

When he heard the water come on a few seconds later, Gianni couldn't stop where his mind went. The images of Laney in the stall, steam billowing around her bare skin as she lathered soap all over herself.

Only a slim door separated them. What would

happen if he knocked on that door? Asked her exactly what she thought about the notion of him coming in, joining her?

Whoa. Steady there, fella.

He blinked hard and forced the pictures away. He really didn't need the tempting image of her undressed and in the shower. Looked like he wasn't going to need much hot water when it was his turn to shower.

In the meantime, he had to get out of the suite and clear his mind. Some fishy harbor air would do just the trick.

CHAPTER SEVEN

GIANNI HAD BEEN RIGHT. The shower did make her feel loads better. Laney secured the belt of the complimentary terry cloth robe at her waist and wrapped a thick Turkish towel around her wet hair.

When she returned to the suite to tell him the bathroom was all his, he was nowhere to be found. A split second of panic rushed through her center at the thought that he might have changed his mind about the whole thing and just abandoned her. But then she noticed his bags were still sitting on the floor by the coffee table. The rush of relief had her actually chuckling out loud. She should have known better.

Everything she'd witnessed about the man so far had shown him to be honorable and true to his word. There was a lot there to admire. Which was the entire problem, wasn't it?

Gianni was assuming her nerves and anxiety could all be attributed to the show they were about to perform for her family. He was only partly right. Another very large piece of the puzzle as far as her nervousness went was the way she reacted to the man whenever they were together. Never before had she felt so drawn to another person. And it was more than just physical.

But this was no time to even consider or even acknowledge any kind of romantic feelings. She still felt emotionally bruised and battered from being dumped so unceremoniously by the man she was convinced would be proposing on the trip they'd been about to embark on. Hah! She couldn't have been more wrong.

Oh, and there was also the whole fact that Gianni hadn't shown even the slightest indication that he was feeling at all the same way toward her. Aside from a few charmingly quaint compliments.

No, she couldn't risk being so ridiculously incorrect yet again. Her pride wouldn't be able to take it. Nor would her heart.

A knock on the door pulled her out of her musings. Had Gianni forgotten his key? When she peeped through the eyehole, a different familiar face greeted her.

Mabel, her cousin.

A smile instantly formed on Laney's face. Mabel was always fun and pleasant company. And she was a sweetheart. Though three years younger, Mabel always seemed so wise and enlightened. Laney could really use some of that right now.

She opened the door without hesitation.

"Hey, coz!" Mabel threw her arms around her shoulders and Laney enthusiastically returned the hug.

"I'm so glad to see you!" They both spoke over each other, saying the same thing.

"How was the trip up from Vermont?" Mable was doing graduate work at UVM in a very demanding biology program. Which meant Laney didn't get to see her favorite Taytum nearly often enough.

"I came up yesterday to give myself an extra day. You know how much I love shopping in Boston."

"Find any good bargains?"

Mabel nodded with enthusiasm. "You know it!" She took Laney by the hand and led her to one of the loveseats. "Never mind that. Are you alone?"

Laney nodded. "For now. My date appears to have stepped out."

"Good," Mabel decreed. "You and I need to have a chat."

Uh-oh, Laney could just imagine what this was about. And she wasn't sure if she was quite prepared for it just yet. Mabel was no doubt about to serve up a third-degree-level questioning about the new mystery man Laney was bringing to a monumental family event. She had to find a way to stall. Pointing to her head and robe, she began to argue. "I should really get dressed first."

Mabel held firm, by literally not releasing Laney's hand. "You can do that later. Right now, it's time for you to spill."

Laney started to argue, then stopped short. Perhaps talking to Mabel for a few minutes was just what the doctor ordered. Who better for a practice run than the dear and kindhearted cousin she'd always felt so affectionate toward? In fact, under any other circumstances, she'd confide fully in the other woman. But she just couldn't risk the very real possibility that Mabel would let something slip to the wrong person. She was definitely a talker.

"Tell me all about the new man in your life," Mabel said. "And I can't believe what that low-life Joseph pulled."

Laney waited for the hurt and outrage that she expected to wash over her when the topic of Joseph came up.

Surprisingly, it simply wasn't there.

What did that mean, that she was over him so quickly? All she felt was a low-level anger at having been treated with such disregard.

"I'd rather not talk about Joseph. Or so much

as think about him," she said, realizing perhaps for the first time just how true those words were.

Mabel nodded. "Fine by me. Emily told me you were with someone new. But she didn't know much about him."

Laney made sure not to rush. She had to tread carefully and avoid saying anything that might trip her up later. Or Gianni, for that matter. She had to stick to the thought-out script they'd agreed on.

"He's great, May. I can't wait for you to meet him."

Mabel's grin grew wider. "Me too! Where is he?"

"He must have stepped out for a bit."

"Then tell me all about him. What can I expect?"

"He's like no one I've ever met." Laney felt a warmth spread through her chest as she said the words.

For it was the absolute truth.

When Gianni returned to the suite about twenty minutes later, he didn't need to open the door to know that Laney wasn't alone. The distinct sound of two different female voices floated through the wooden doorway. Though he had his room key, he knocked in order to announce his arrival.

The door opened within seconds. Laney stood across the threshold in a white fluffy robe that looked about three sizes too big and an even fluffier towel wrapped around her head.

She looked downright adorable.

His hands itched to unwrap the towel and let her hair fall over her shoulders, then to run his fingers through the wet strands. He wanted so badly to remove the robe and discover exactly what lay beneath the fabric. So much so, he forgot there was someone else there with her. He took a deep breath to dislodge the wayward thoughts. Then he caught sight of a petite blonde with wispy hair and bright hazel eyes sitting on the sofa. She gave him a small wave and a big smile. The eye color told him she had to be a relative.

"Hey there," he said to Laney, not sure what to do. Should he give her a kiss or something? Hadn't they talked about this very thing? If so, for the life of him, he couldn't remember. In his defense, he hadn't been expecting his first introduction to be a surprise visitor to the suite.

"Just went out for some fresh air," he told Laney, trying to ask her the question silently with his eyes.

It didn't work. Laney stepped aside to let him in. "Did you forget your key?"

"No. Sounded like you weren't alone and I didn't want to intrude."

Both eyebrows lifted and she gave him a dazzling smile, as if he'd passed some sort of test. "See," Laney threw over her shoulder at the other woman. "What did I tell you? He's so considerate." She gave him a small wink. "Come meet my cousin."

The blonde immediately stood and strode to where they both stood.

"Gianni, this is Mabel. Mabel, meet Gianni," Laney said as she shut the door.

Gianni extended his hand, but it was bypassed as the cousin reached with both arms to grip him in a tight hug. So this was clearly one of the few who didn't fit the mold. She was about the furthest thing from standoffish as he could think of.

"It's so nice to meet you," she was saying under his chin. "We're so glad you're here with Laney."

Gianni waited to speak until she let go. To his amusement, it took several beats.

"Thank you. I'm very glad to be here."

To his surprise, Laney took his hand in hers. He had to work hard at not reacting to her unexpected touch. How silly of him to be so affected when he knew full well the gesture was purely for show in front of her cousin.

"Mabel's working on her doctorate in animal science. She's studying to be a veterinarian, specializing in marine animals," Laney explained.

So this one was an academic, as well.

"Keeps her very busy," Laney added. "I haven't seen her in months."

"Then I should leave you two to your visit."

"Oh, no," Mabel protested. "I'm the one who should leave. I need to get ready in any case." She gestured toward Laney with a laugh. "And you do too!"

Without giving himself a chance to think, Gianni pulled Laney up against him, tight to his side. "I think she looks adorable."

He felt her shock as she stiffened next to him. She recovered quickly. She stepped fully into his embrace, wrapped his arms around her waist with her back up against his front. "Oh, he's such a charmer, isn't he?"

Mabel stood grinning at them both. Looked like they were pretty convincing. "I'd say."

"It's easy to be charming with you, *cara mia*," he told her, at the risk of laying it on a bit thick. Throwing the Italian in there might have been a bit much. But it was hard to deny that he was enjoying this—the affectionate banter between the two of them…the feel of Laney in his arms.

If only they didn't have an audience. Which was a silly thought. After all, that was the entire point, wasn't it?

Mabel looked ready to swoon at the sight they made.

He leaned closer to give her a small peck on

the cheek. Laney chose that very moment to tilt her head up and back to look at him. They somehow met in the middle. He didn't allow himself to think. He meant to give her a small peck, just to complete the charade, but his mouth seemed to have different intentions. Before he knew what was happening, his lips were on hers. He couldn't even tell which one of them started it.

She tasted exactly as he'd imagined she would. Like the sweetest fruit at its most ripe. Like cream and honey and nectar all in one. He breathed in her scent as he tasted her. A small moan sounded from her mouth into his.

It was over all too soon.

Laney pulled away with a jolt, no doubt remembering there was another individual in the room with them. A fact he'd so easily forgotten.

Mabel had her hands clasped to her chest, studying them with a clearly heartfelt smile. She actually said, "Aw. How sweet." As if she'd just watched a scene from a holiday movie on one of those seasonal channels.

Somehow, when he wasn't looking, he'd found himself playing leading man.

She should have found a way to stop the kiss. Or she should have managed somehow to avoid it altogether for it had left her shaken to the core. If Gianni had been moved by it in any way, there was no sign of it in his expression or his manner. And why should there be? He'd done it simply for show. He'd behaved exactly as she'd asked him to around her family members. She was the one being silly.

Someone in the room cleared their throat. She couldn't be sure, but it might have even been her. Right. They weren't alone. This was just pretend. The kiss that had so shaken her was merely a ruse, a playact. Nothing more. So she'd do well to ignore the quaking sensation in her middle.

"I guess I'll see you both aboard the boat, then," Mabel said as she started walking toward the door. "So nice to have finally met you, Gianni."

"Likewise," he answered, his voice steady and cheery. Not shaky at all, unlike her. She was right. He hadn't been affected by the kiss in the least. Had probably already forgotten about it. What a fool she could be when it came to men in general and to Gianni in particular. How many times could she leave her heart unguarded only to have it bruised?

She didn't bring herself to glance at him as she turned toward the bedroom once Mabel had left. "I guess I'll finally go get dressed. Be out soon."

"I'll be here."

By the time she came out dressed and ready twenty minutes later, she'd managed to steady herself and had only thought about his lips on hers about a dozen more times. Progress. Her dress of choice for the occasion was a silk wrap in a deep navy blue. A color that always seemed to complement her despite her dark coloring and olive skin tone. If she were being fanciful, she could swear Gianni did a bit of a double take when she emerged fully dressed and heeled. The idea had her nearly giddy and she made sure to squash it with haste.

For his part, Gianni had changed into a fresh collared shirt and beige khakis. He somehow seemed to make the casual outfit look stylish and elegant. He could have been a picture out of a magazine cologne ad spread. The man certainly cleaned up well. As if he weren't attractive enough in simple jeans and a T-shirt. Or even a waist apron.

"Ready to go?" he asked.

"As ready as I'll ever be."

They were outside and walking toward the harbor marina within minutes. The afternoon was mild and warm, sunlight filtering through thick white clouds. One had to hand it to Emily. She somehow managed to book a day in which the weather couldn't have been more ideally suited for a city cruise.

Laney exhaled a deep breath once they approached the vessel's boarding ramp. The happy notes of party music sounded in the air. The DJ had started with a bouncy new pop song that featured an accompanying dance. Laney heard the sound of a cork popping. "I guess this is it. The moment we've been prepping for. Ready to meet my people?"

"Ready and able, Captain." He gestured toward the ramp.

A crew member greeted them at the entry way and asked for their names, which she then crossed off a list.

"Go right on up," she instructed, her smile bright and cheery. "You're not late but the party is well underway."

"That's not a bad way to sum up my life in general," Laney found herself saying as they made their way toward the hub.

"What's that?"

"I'm not often late but somehow the party has always started without me," she explained with a small chuckle. But Gianni wasn't smiling when she glanced over at him.

"Do you really see yourself that way?"

She'd meant it as a small joke. Though now that he was asking, she realized how true the statement was.

She gave a small shrug as she answered him. "I guess I do. I always feel like those around me have moved on as I'm perpetually trying to catch up." It could certainly be said about her last relationship, in fact. "I seem to be the square peg in the round hole all too often."

He stopped in his tracks. "I haven't known you that long, but I don't see you that way at all."

"You don't?"

"No. Not in the least."

She was afraid to ask the next question but mustered the courage to do so. "Then how do you see me?"

Something shifted behind his eyes. Something she didn't want to analyze too deeply. "You're bright. You're successful. Fun to be around. As far as catching up to others, have you ever considered that you might just be going in a different direction?"

"Not really."

He inhaled a quick breath. "You chose a different path than the family of attorneys you come from. That says nothing about your accomplishments or success. It merely says you decided to pursue your own goals."

"Guess I hadn't thought of it that way."

"Maybe you should start," he said, then slowly started walking again. Laney didn't move with him right away. Instead, she let the full impact of his words really settle in. Not just the last part, though the statement about her going in a different direction was certainly something to think about. She'd always been the square peg in her family.

But everything he had said before that echoed through her head. He thought she was bright. And fun. Which implied he liked being with her. That he actually enjoyed her company. Given the way Joseph had dumped her a couple weeks ago, the thought that this much more dynamic and alluring man felt that way made for a heady feeling. She'd be lying if she didn't say she felt flattered and…well, validated.

Suddenly, the next forty-eight hours didn't seem so daunting. Not with Gianni by her side. She'd be able to get through this. His words had somehow given her a shot of confidence—something she hadn't felt in a while.

Gianni seemed to finally realize she hadn't kept step with him. He turned and gave her a questioning look. "Coming?"

"I just need a minute."

"Still nervous?"

She wasn't really. Thanks to him. "I just want to gather my thoughts before we venture into the crowd."

"That's fair."

She strolled over to the rail, the sounds of the party still echoing through the air around them. Gianni joined her, and for several moments they remained silent, simply taking in the view of the Boston skyline from the water.

"Also, I just wanted to thank you," Laney eventually said.

"For coming with you? Already told you. I'm just here to enjoy a party with a beautiful woman."

He was doing so much more than that. She shuddered to think what the day ahead of her might have looked like if she'd had to endure it solo. All the questions about why she was there alone. Of course, now there were bound to be questions about the new man she was with. But those would be so much easier to answer with someone by her side.

Even if it was all a lie.

CHAPTER EIGHT

"YOUR DAD KEEPS staring at me."

Gianni took a sip from his frosty bottle of beer and made sure to keep his polite smile in place. The introductions so far had been short and sweet, with Laney's parents assuring him they'd make time later for a longer chat after the wedding tomorrow, when there would be less distractions. Or maybe *threatening* would be a better word to use in this context.

"Don't sweat it," Laney said, swirling her glass of Chardonnay absentmindedly as they sat at one of the side tables. "He's just trying to measure you up a bit."

He had to chuckle at that. "And I'm not supposed to sweat it that he's doing so?"

The soiree was fully underway now. They were past the harbor waters and the city skyline was well off in the distance. Emily had gone all out and chartered a tri-deck luxury yacht with tinted glass walls and a plush luxurious interior big enough to house a dance floor, ample number of tables for guests, and comfy sofas and upholstered chairs for the close to three-hundred guests in attendance. True to form, Emily had succeeded in securing the perfect venue for her first wedding event.

Laney shrugged before answering Gianni's question. "It's not like it really matters, does it? Eventually, we'll have to tell them that you're not in my life anymore."

It was silly of him to feel any kind of offense to what she said, but he did, nonetheless. Funny, up until she'd spoken the words, he hadn't realized just how much he did want to remain a part of her life, in some shape or form. Which might be hard if she wasn't keen on selling her business.

She was right. This was not the time for him to worry about how the business deal might play out or what type of friendship the future might have in store for them. Though, the way she looked in the silky sky blue wrap dress she wore, friendship wasn't exactly the first thing that came to mind. His mouth had gone dry when she'd first walked out of the bedroom wearing it. His skin still itched with the desire to run his fingers over the silky material. If he allowed himself, he could so easily imagine helping her out of it and then carrying her away behind a closed door.

Before he could reprimand himself for those

thoughts, a small child darted out from behind a table and practically jumped onto Laney's lap. "Hi, Aun' Wainey."

Laney immediately cuddled the toddler closer to her chest and gave her a peck on the cheek. "Well, hello, pumpkin. I was wondering where you were."

Pumpkin pulled her thumb out of her mouth and pointed at him. "Who dat?"

"This is my very good friend. His name is Gianni."

"Jownee?"

He had to laugh at the pronunciation. "And what might your name be?" he asked.

"I'm Lisbeth."

"Nice to meet you, Lisbeth."

Laney tousled the girl's hair. "Lisbeth is my little cousin. Mabel's niece."

"Yeah? I have a niece," he said, for the benefit of them both, but Lisbeth had already lost interest in them. She left Laney's lap and scampered off without so much as a glance back.

"She's cute as a button," he told Laney when the child had skipped off toward the dance floor. A tall man with blond hair scooped her up in his arms and twirled her around to the music.

"That she is," Laney answered. "With the attention span of the three-year-old toddler that she is. How old is your niece?"

"Not much older. She just turned four. Her brother is younger by about two years."

"You're an uncle, times two?"

"I am indeed. I make sure to spoil them rotten."

She laughed and took a sip of her wine. "Oh, their parents must love that."

"It's no less than what my brother deserves, the way he annoyed me when we were kids. I finally get some payback."

"Revenge by spoiling his kids. Diabolical."

"Yep. And just as they're about to throw the inevitable tantrum, I simply hand them back to Mom and Dad and make my escape."

She held her wine glass up and tipped it toward him. "There's one thing you might not have thought of in all of this."

"What's that?"

"What happens when your brother and his spouse get their own chance at revenge? Like once you have kids of your own?"

Her question was an innocent enough one. But it wasn't one worth entertaining. He'd decided long ago he wasn't the type to play husband or daddy. He had no intention of having a family of his own. Falling in love and having kids weren't for him. Love could make a man swallow his pride so hard that he could pretend the world wasn't laughing at him when it clearly was. Just look at his own pop.

"That's not going to happen," he answered, signaling the server for another beer. "I don't plan on having kids of my own. A family man, I'm not."

She narrowed her eyes on him. "Oh? Why is that?"

He shrugged. "Just not for me."

"That sounds like a vague way to tell me you don't want to really discuss the subject."

A petite brunette waitress stopped by the table with his drink. "There's really nothing to discuss."

"Consider the matter dropped. It's really none of my business."

The conversation was starting to get too deep, and a heavy mood had suddenly settled in the air between them. Gianni didn't like it. Coupled with the repeated speculative looks Laney's father kept sending him, it was all making him edgy and uncomfortable. He needed to step away from this conversation and from the table. He needed a physical outlet.

He stood and extended his hand to her. "Dance with me."

Laney didn't hesitate. Setting her wineglass down on the table, she stood and took his hand. "About time, Mr. Martino. I thought you'd never ask."

Huh. "Why didn't you just ask me yourself?"

She gave a small shrug of her shoulder. "I

didn't see you dancing at all that night at the club. I thought maybe you were one of those men who lack rhythm or skill." A hint of a smile tugged at the corner of her mouth. She was teasing him.

"You insult me. I can manage a few dance steps." He pulled her gently to the dance floor. "As you are about to find out."

They moved well together. Laney matched him step for step, moving in tune to the music. The image had his mind flashing back to the day he'd witnessed her instructing the exercise class in her club. And it was no less tempting now than it had been then.

Only now they were in the company of a literal boatful of her family and friends, which made such thoughts beyond inappropriate on his part.

It didn't help matters when the song switched over and the next number was a slow and sultry one that happened to have lyrics loaded with sensual undertones.

Laney stepped closer to him, a question deep in the depths of her sparkling amber eyes. He pulled her into his arms without a second thought.

Then he didn't allow himself to think at all.

Laney could only guess the number of eyes that had to be on them. She didn't care. After all, this is what they were after, wasn't it? To put on a show of affection. To look as if they were two lovebirds who had just discovered each other and couldn't get enough.

She sucked in a shaky breath. The scary part was that it was so perilously close to being true on her part. She really was growing rather fond of her pretend boyfriend. A shudder ran over her skin as she recalled their kiss in the room earlier. The taste of his lips on hers still lingered, the tingling sensation in the pit of her stomach resurfaced. The pleasure of being in his arms right now as they swayed slowly to the music. Yeah, no doubt about it, she couldn't exactly deny her developing feelings or her ever-growing attraction.

So what was she going to do about it?

Though she knew the risk, knew fully well the hit her soul would take if he wasn't as attracted to her as she was to him, the way she felt right now in Gianni's arms made all of that moot. Sometimes a girl just had to take a chance.

"Do you remember what I told you about my breakup?" she asked, blurting out the words and clearly surprising him with the question.

He faltered his step ever so slightly but quickly recovered. "Not particularly. Though I was rather hoping we didn't have to discuss the ex as I'm holding you in my arms during a slow dance."

Did that mean he had feelings for her that perhaps bordered on jealousy? But his next words quickly relieved her of that assumption. "It's not really great for my male ego." Just his pride speaking, then.

She shook her head. "This isn't really about him. It's about me."

He continued to lead her through the dance, but his attention and gaze was fully focused on her face now. "Oh?"

"I was told I was boring. What do you think that means?"

He tilted his head, studying her. "I think it means he was a brainless, inconsiderate buffoon who didn't know what he had."

She wasn't going to let the compliments go to her head. Gianni was a charmer. It seemed to be an intrinsic part of his personality. She couldn't take his words to heart, even if he thought he meant them. "No, I mean, why do you think he used that particular description?"

His hold on her seemed to tighten. "I couldn't venture to guess, Laney. But does it really matter?"

It did matter to her. It had stung to hear that description about her coming from someone she thought had loved and cherished her. Someone she thought was getting ready to propose. While she'd thought she may have found someone in

Joseph who finally loved her and respected her for who she was, he'd ultimately rejected her for someone else.

Gianni leaned his face closer to hers. She could feel his warm breath on her cheek, along her neck. The sensation sent a shiver of longing through her core.

"I thought we established he was just making excuses."

Excuses to justify rejecting her. To toss her aside without guilt.

Gianni continued, "He described you in a way that was a much more fitting description of himself."

Yet that was too simple of an explanation. "Hmm. Maybe."

He sighed. "You don't sound convinced. I see no reason to give it any more thought. Unless... do you still have feelings for him?" he asked, nearly whispering the words. She might have been imagining the rasp in his voice.

"No. Not in any real sense. More a feeling of disappointment in what I thought was real that clearly wasn't."

"So why the questions?"

"I'm just trying to understand. When someone tells you you're boring, that typically means you're afraid to take chances, that you're scared of making a mistake." It was so hard to search for the exact right words. She had to do better. "That you're afraid of asking for what you want for fear of rejection."

An eyebrow raised in question. "Where exactly are you going with this?"

"I guess I'm asking for what I want. Regardless of the consequences." *I want you.*

He inhaled a deep breath and then let it out slowly. "You're going to have to be really clear here, sweetheart. I don't want to be making any kind of incorrect assumptions. Not about something like this."

Maybe she was making a mistake here. One she might regret later. After all, it had been a long day and she'd had more than one glass of wine. Still, at this moment, what she was about to do felt right. And she wouldn't question it any further. Perhaps it was indeed time she simply lived for the moment.

She wanted what she wanted. And she wasn't going to deny herself. "Then I guess I'll spell it out in concrete terms. I'd like to go back to the room soon. And I don't want you to sleep on the couch. Nor do I want you to drive back home."

If he was about to reject her, to tell her what she was saying made no sense, or that they barely knew each other, then so be it. She would find out once and for all that the attraction was one-sided and solely on her part. At least that way she would know that she hadn't chickened out. That she'd taken her shot and gotten her answer.

"I see. And exactly what *do* you want?" The thickness in his voice was unmistakable this time.

"I'd like you to stay the night. With me."

Gianni could tell by looking in her eyes what it must have taken for her to speak those words out loud. She couldn't have any idea the effect hearing them had on him now. His heart pounded wildly in his chest. The urge to lift her in his arms and carry her back to the hotel had his muscles twitching. Somehow, he managed to contain himself to keep from doing just that.

He had to try and think straight here, hard as that was to do. After all, he'd known, hadn't he? All the previous moments of desire and longing had led them here to this very point in time. He couldn't deny that he'd seen it coming.

Laney squeezed her eyes shut and bit out a mild curse. "Oh, no. I've really stepped in it this time, haven't I?"

She'd taken his hesitation as rejection. How far from the truth…

"Gianni, I'm so sorry. Look, if you don't want—"

He silenced her with a press of his finger to her lips. "Don't even think about finishing that sentence." She honestly thought he might not want her. There was no way he could let her think that for even so much as a moment. It was so far from the truth.

She slowly opened her eyes to look back up at him. "Why?"

"You beautiful, silly fool."

A long and slow sigh escaped her lips. "I thought maybe… Does that mean you want this too?"

How in the world could he say no? It would be such a big lie.

He glanced around the room to see who was left still partying. Unfortunately, all the important family members still seemed to be lingering about. As expected, Laney's dad was even at this moment eyeing the two of them. Gianni knew he should care, but he couldn't bring himself to. "How fast can you say your goodbyes?"

Within moments, they were off the boat and onto the harbor walkway. Gianni couldn't seem to let go of her, his arm around her waist, half carrying her.

She pulled him to a stop under a streetlight, turning him to face her. "I want you to know, this isn't characteristic of me."

"You don't have to explain yourself, Laney."

Her lips tightened. "It's just that I want you to understand. I don't typically ask for what I want. There's just something about you."

He tightened his hold around her. "Then I'm honored to have triggered the transformation."

Her response was to pull his face to hers. The kiss sent a surge of pure pleasure down his chest clear to his toes. For several moments, he just let himself indulge, to take her in fully, to taste the sweetness she was offering. Still, there were things he needed to say. Confessions he needed to make to her.

He forced himself to pull away.

"Listen, Laney. Before we—"

The sound of a loud giggle behind them interrupted his speech. "Get a room," yelled a feminine voice with a teasing, amused tone.

Laney gave the stranger a small nod before turning back to him. "I think she's right. We should get to our room." She took him by the hand and led him toward the hotel. The time it took to get from the sidewalk up to their room seemed to take forever. Finally, Laney swiped the keycard and they were through the door.

Now. He had to tell her now.

But she immediately wrapped her arms around him as soon as they shut the door behind them. Gianni could barely manage more than a low growl of pleasure as her lips found his once again.

He started to speak against her mouth. "Laney, about that night at your club."

She shook her head, continued kissing him. She whispered softly against his lips, "Mr. Martino, I was really hoping to keep the conversation to a minimum."

The thickness of her voice, the sheer longing woven through her tone was his final undoing. When she eventually broke the kiss and took him by the hand to lead him to the bedroom, he could do nothing but follow.

So this was what all the romantic books and movies had been referring to. Laney slowly opened her eyes as thin rays of morning sunlight filtered through the blinds of the large bay window across the bed. She felt languid, more relaxed than she'd felt in a long time.

Images from the night before flooded her mind and she felt heat throughout her entire body.

She was going to take the memory of last night and cherish it for the rest of her life. The way she'd been held last night, the way Gianni had loved her and held and whispered sweetly in her ear, the way he'd simply made her *feel* was an experience she would never forget.

What did it matter that it was only a fling?

She felt him rustle next to her just as a set of warm, gentle arms wrapped around her waist and pulled her closer up against him, her back to his chest. Hard to believe just how right it felt to be lying next to him in his arms.

"Why are you awake? It's got to be early still," he asked softly against her ear before trailing a line of kisses along her cheek, down her jaw and to her neck.

A small purr of pleasure escaped her lips. She could get used to this.

Except she really couldn't. This was just one weekend. A simple fling. After the wedding was over, they'd both go their separate ways. Gianni had given absolutely zero indication that he was after anything permanent. Look how disdainful he'd been last night when talk had turned to family.

She squeezed her eyes shut. She had no business even thinking the word. For one, she had some serious thinking to do herself about exactly what she wanted for herself in the future. There was no way she was ready for any kind of other relationship so soon.

Moot point. She was getting way ahead of herself.

Funny, she'd never considered herself to be the type to indulge in a no-strings-attached fling, but she'd never encountered the likes of Gianni Martino before.

"I was thinking about calling room service," she answered his question once she could find her breath and her focus. His hands were doing very distracting things at the moment. “I for one could use a strong pot of coffee.”

“Yeah? Didn’t get much sleep last night, did we?” he said with a rather naughty hitch to his voice. It had her giggling like a schoolgirl in response. His lips found hers again and she allowed her hands to roam over the toned muscles of his arms the way she had last night. She couldn’t seem to get enough of touching him.

It was much later until they got around to ordering the coffee.

To her delight, Gianni had thought to order a variety tray of pastries and spreads. Dressed in the terry robe again, she tucked her feet under her on the loveseat as she bit into a rich buttery croissant. A steaming cup of Boston dark roast sat on the coffee table beside her.

The cushion shifted as Gianni plopped down next to her. He ate what remained of a cinnamon roll that had originally been the size of a small dinner plate.

“So, how did I do yesterday? Does your family think I’m good enough for you?”

“Wrong question.”

“Again, huh? I seem to keep doing that.”

She patted his knee. “You are still learning,” she announced in a wise sage voice.

He gave a slight chuckle. "What's the right question, then?"

"Whether they think you're good enough for *them.* And they're still deciding by the way." It pulled her up short when she realized how that must have sounded. "I'm sorry. I know that's not really fair."

He took another bite of his breakfast treat. "No problem. I like a challenge." He certainly had a healthy ego. Good thing too. He would need it to get through the rest of the ceremonies, which included an early lunch followed by the wedding vows and finally the reception.

"To answer your question. You couldn't have done any better, as far as I'm concerned."

"Yeah?" He polished off the rest of his pastry in one big bite. "You think so?"

"I do. You were quite charming, a big hit with both ladies and gents alike. And toddlers. Lisbeth seemed taken by you as well by the end of the night."

He grinned at her. "Charming happens to be my middle name."

"Well, it fits."

So did he. He really had fit in yesterday with a group of people he'd only just met. She really had to thank her lucky stars. Central casting at a major movie studio couldn't have picked a better candidate for whom she needed by her side this weekend.

To think he'd just walked into her life at the perfect time.

Just when she'd needed him.

What a mess he'd gotten himself into.

Gianni tried to keep the mood light and amusing for Laney's sake as they ate their breakfast. But inside he was full of conflict. It was tearing him up inside that he was keeping such a big truth from her.

Now, as he listened to her humming while she showered, he cursed in frustration.

He had come perilously close to the precipice of spilling the entire truth to her last night. But the way Laney had told him that she wanted to be with him, the way she'd asked him to stay with her had made it impossible to find any kind of feasible way to even bring up the subject.

What was he supposed to say?

The reason I was even in your club two weeks ago was because I work for the family business and we'd like to buy you out. Now, where were we?

Not exactly pillow talk. And how could he possibly tell her now? He wouldn't be able to live with himself if he ruined her sister's wedding for her. The only reason he was here was to make things easier for Laney with her loved ones. Nothing would change if he kept the truth from her a little longer.

As for last night, he'd like to think that had been inevitable, meant to be. From the moment he'd laid eyes on her, something deep within him had known they'd become intimate. Nothing had been going to stop what happened between him and Laney last night. The moment they met, they were drawn to each other in a way that couldn't be deterred.

No. He would have to find a better time to tell her the truth once this weekend was over. Surely, he'd be able to make her see where he was coming from. Business was business. Personal was personal. As a business owner herself, she had to understand that their personal relationship had nothing to do with any offer he may present her with in the future.

He realized now he'd missed the best opportunity he'd had to tell her. The night she'd come over for dinner, he should have come clean. He'd just been enjoying her company so much he'd actually almost forgotten the circumstances surrounding their first meeting.

Well, there was no use dwelling on mistakes of the past. It wouldn't do him any good now. Now he had to focus on the best way to make things right and exactly how to do it. Laney was a reasonable woman. She'd accept his apologies for misleading her.

He could only hope he wasn't being overly and naively optimistic.

CHAPTER NINE

THE WEDDING WAS a big hit. Couldn't have gone better, in fact. A beautiful ceremony had commenced into a massive reception at the grand ballroom of the Boston Harbor Hotel. Aside from sitting down to the gourmet dinner of braised salmon with sautéed root vegetables and fluffy whipped potatoes drizzled with truffle oil, she and Gianni had spent most of the evening on the dance floor. Despite what he'd told her that night at the club, he was a more than competent dancer. Laney had long ago kicked off her heels and removed her bulky gold leaf earrings. A slight sheen of perspiration covered her forehead and the back of her neck.

She was enjoying herself.

Sure, she had plenty of opportunity to dance in her daily life. Owning a nightclub meant it was a large part of the job description, but those times were more of a responsibility, a performance to wrangle clients onto the dance floor if it was too empty for too long. Tonight was different. She couldn't remember the last time she'd danced just for fun, for the sheer joy that moving her body to music brought to her soul.

Now, Gianni twirled her around in a semicircle before dipping her dramatically when the music hit a crescendo as the song ended. She couldn't help the girlish giggle that escaped her lips.

The DJ chose that moment to announce he was taking what had to be a much-needed break. As the music came to a stop and the lights in the ballroom turned up brighter, she leaned into Gianni. "You know, you lied to me the night we met," she teased.

Something shifted behind his yes. "I did?"

She gave an emphatic nod. "You told me you weren't much of a dancer."

He blinked. "Oh, that."

What else did he think she might be referring to? Before she had a chance to ask, he gently took her by the elbow and led her off the dance floor back to their table. "I could use a drink. Can I get you more wine?" he asked.

"Yes, please."

Laney watched as Gianni made his way to the bar. Several of the groomsmen and guests stopped him to chat. Gianni had fit in rather well with the rest of the wedding party. The groomsmen treated him like he'd known them all for ages. His knowledge of kickboxing and the fact that he co-owned a string of gyms had broken the ice quickly with the other men. Including her new brother-in-law. Plus, Gianni had an easy manner that had also helped to acclimate him with the others.

Was there anything the man wasn't good at?

She gave her head a brisk shake. She was dangerously on the verge of becoming besotted. And that would be perilous indeed. Despite their night of intimacy, they hardly knew each other. Though that was changing by the minute.

"Please explain to me what's happened, Elaine." Her mom's voice interrupted her thoughts. Laney looked up to find her parents pulling out the empty chairs at her table. They both sat down and turned to face her head on.

Uh-oh. She'd been caught unaware. Too focused on Gianni, she hadn't even seen them approach. But then again, her parents had a way of being stealth-like, particularly when it came to keeping their girls in check.

It was time for the Gianni third-degree grilling. Nothing she could do about it now.

She really had wished to put it off a while longer. She took a deep calming breath and prepared herself for the onslaught.

"What do you mean?"

Her mother pinched her lips before answering. "I'd think it was obvious. You were on the verge of being engaged yourself to Joseph. And now you're with someone else entirely. Tell me again, how exactly did all that happen so fast? What in the world is going on with you?"

"Now, now, dear," her dad said, patting his wife's hand gently on the table. "This probably isn't the time or place. We are here to enjoy Emily's nuptials." Laney hadn't fully released her sigh of relief when her father turned his intense gaze on her. "But your mother's right. You owe us some answers, young lady."

"It just seems so sudden," her mother continued, without so much as giving Laney a chance to respond. "Why, he's practically a stranger."

Laney cut her off before she could continue with that train of thought. "It's okay, Mom, Dad. You don't have to worry. We're taking things slow." She had to look away as she uttered the last word as memories of their night together rushed through her head. That was just physical. Not that she'd be sharing that bit of knowledge with present company.

"Good," Mom declared. "I'm glad to hear it."

"What does he do again?" her father asked, studying Gianni as he slowly made his way back to the table.

Laney caught his eyes, trying to send him an apologetic look. His shrug was almost imperceptible, but she caught the slight motion. Her father waved him over.

Don't panic. All is fine.

They'd planned for this moment, after all. Hardly unexpected. Truth be told, she was surprised it had taken her parents as long as it had.

Gianni approached with a friendly smile and was at their table in no time. Charming as ever, he gave her mom a nod first, then shook her father's hand after setting her wineglass down in front of her. He sat down in the remaining empty chair.

"Finally," her father began without any kind of pretense. "A chance to talk."

Laney tried to give Gianni a reassuring smile, but he didn't seem fazed in the least, just sat there calmly sipping his beer before he answered. "Likewise. Laney told me so much about you when we first met. And Emily. You're a lovely family."

Whoa, fella. Try not to spread it on too thick.

Her mom leaned closer, resting her arms on the table. "Thank you. That's a lovely thing to say." She scrunched her face. "We're looking forward to getting to know you better."

Very subtle, Mom. A nice, roundabout way to tell him they didn't know him that well. And they intended to change that fact as fast as possible.

"We were inquiring what it is that you do for a living," her father supplied. The tag team was in full practice now.

"I'm a managing VP for Martino Entertainment Enterprises," Gianni answered. "My father founded the company as a young man upon his arrival to the States three decades ago."

"Martino Entertainment Enterprises. That sounds familiar," her father said, his eyebrows drawn together in thought.

"We own and manage various fitness and entertainment venues. Everything from boxing gyms to gaming halls to smaller casinos."

"Ah, yes," her father responded. "Now it's ringing a bell. I read somewhere you're looking to expand."

Was it her imagination or did Gianni flinch ever so slightly? "Always," he answered with after another swig of his beer. "Got to grow the business. At all costs," he added almost under his breath with another swig of his beer. She might not have heard him if she weren't hyper-focused on the conversation.

He hadn't told her much about his business. Or his family, for that matter. But clearly there was a story there. Maybe he'd feel comfortable enough with her at some point in the future to confide what that story might be.

Gianni hadn't meant to say that last part out loud. Judging by the way she was looking at him, Laney had definitely heard him. Luckily, her father changed the subject. “It’s rather lucky, isn’t it? That you two met when you did.”

Yeah, the new subject matter could be considered equally full of landmines. “Laney tells me you were visiting the club one night, even though you’d never been there before.”

He gave her a sideways smile. “Guess it was meant to be.” Man, when he finally told her the full story, there was going to be so much explaining he needed to do.

“Yes, I’m glad she managed a plus-one to the wedding, after all,” her mother added. Laney’s cheeks were growing redder by the second. “Now, she just needs to figure out what to do about this trip to Italy she planned. Positano, then Florence, already paid for.” She patted her daughter’s hand, but there was zero affection in the gesture. “Yet another impulsive decision on your part that seems to have bitten you in the hind. I don’t suppose you can get your money back.”

“I have every intention of going still, Mother. Gianni might even come with me.”

Whoa. He hadn’t seen that coming. Laney looked ready to slide under the table. Clearly, she’d said it without much thought.

He wasn’t sure what to say. This whole conversation was throwing him off. He just wanted to somehow get the look of utter despair off Laney’s face. He had family in Positano. "I have a great aunt and several cousins in that area. Positano."

Why had he thrown out that fact? It sounded like he was considering actually going with her. Of course, that was out of the question.

"Oh?" her mom said. "Where did you say your hotel was again, Laney?"

She hadn't said, as her mother had never actually inquired about the hotel before. "A seaside hotel on the Amalfi Coast. The Palazzo Positano," she answered.

"Is your family in that area, Gianni?" her mom wanted to know.

Before Gianni could respond, Laney jumped in. "I haven't made any final decisions about the trip. Let's just drop it, okay?"

Her mom gave her a sharp look that bordered on pity. "Of course."

Several moments of awkward silence ensued. Gianni had taken gut punches in the ring that had left him feeling more comfortable. Luckily, fate intervened. Laney's mom suddenly stood. "Well, it looks like they're about to cut the cake." She took her husband's hand. "Let's go, dear."

Laney's sigh of relief was audible as they walked away. "I am so sorry, Gianni."

"Nothing to apologize for. That wasn't so bad." That much was true. Up until the whole Italy conversation, he'd been managing pretty well.

"What I said just now, about you traveling with me to Positano, you have to know it was just for their benefit. So they would just drop the subject. I don't really expect you to come to Italy with me."

Ouch. As infeasible as it was, she made it sound like the idea was preposterous. "Yeah. Go figure."

"I guess I should have seen that coming."

"Hey, the good news is, you have a bit of a reprieve from the paternal third degree. And we're about to eat some wedding cake."

Her lips curled up in a smile. "I suppose so. Guess I should look on the bright side, huh? Silver linings and all that."

He tipped his nearly empty bottle in her direction in a mini salute. "Always."

She picked up her glass and touched it to his bottle. "A toast to silver linings. So, have you ever been, then? To Italy? You said you had family there."

The question brought back a flood of memories. Most of them pleasant and joyful. Except for one moment he'd rather forget.

"A few times. I could recommend some places, if you'd like. If you do decide to go, that is."

She studied his face. "Sure, I'd like that."

Something about her expression made him want to pull her onto his lap and wrap his arms around her. In an alternate universe, this conversation could go a completely different way. He wished things were different. That they really were together and he could take this trip of a lifetime with her. He could show her all the sites in Italy he enjoyed, a lover slash tour guide in one. Then he'd have her meet his family.

He had no business even entertaining such thoughts. He was only here with her to play a part, to help her get through her sister's wedding. They weren't exactly a couple in any sense of the word, certainly not one who'd be planning any kind of international trip together. Though he couldn't deny how much it shook him that he wanted to so badly. To travel with her, to show her his Italy.

Moot point. He couldn't very well change reality, could he? As much as he wanted to. So he'd settle for being able to spend one more night with her before it all had to come to an end.

CHAPTER TEN

ONE OF THESE days maybe she'd learn to stop checking her phone for missed messages or missed calls. It appeared today was not that day. Though why she bothered was beyond her. One week since the wedding and Gianni hadn't contacted her other than a perfunctory reply to her one text thanking him for attending with her.

Well, what had she expected?

Gianni had done her a favor that weekend. Nothing more. She'd asked him to help her save face at her sister's wedding and he'd obliged. And he'd done so in a way she'd be eternally grateful for. Maybe if their paths crossed again, they could form some kind of friendship. As for their weekend fling, that was simply two adults enjoying each other's company under some rather uncanny circumstances. Gianni had never alluded differently. And to be completely truthful, neither had she.

So she was going to resist checking her phone yet again this hour. In fact, she was going to set it to silent and not even look at it until the club opened for the evening. Business calls were a completely different number. And heaven knew, she didn't have anything pressing that was personal.

She had a lot to do before she flew to Italy in a few days No time to constantly interrupt herself, looking for messages that weren't there from a man she should just start to forget. Surely, in time, he would stop appearing in her dreams night after night. But she couldn't deny the truth. Gianni Martino was going to be a hard man to forget and put behind her. The way he'd made her feel, the things he'd said to her. Almost as if he saw her in a way no one else had.

With a resigned sigh, Laney fished her phone out of her pocket to change the setting when a dull knock on her office door stopped her.

"Come in."

Her head bartender poked her head in the door. "Hey, boss. Someone here to see you. One Gianni Martino."

Laney's heart gave a thud, then proceeded to pound wildly in her chest. Gianni was here? She couldn't help the thrill that washed over her. He was actually physically here. That was better than any text message or voice mail. Had he missed her as much as she'd missed him? Another exciting possibility occurred to her that sent a lightning bolt through her midsection. What if he'd decided that he wanted to go to Italy with her?

"Oh?"

"I can tell him you're busy. He said he doesn't have an appointment."

"No!" Laney jumped out of her chair, clearly startling the other woman. "I mean, no appointment needed. He's a friend."

When he stepped into her office a moment later, she realized just how inadequate describing him as a friend was. Dressed in a well-cut gray suit that fit him like a glove, he could have been an image out of a commercial. She itched to run over and give him a hug. But something in his manner gave her pause.

"Hey, Laney." It sounded friendly enough, but his smile was off. No warmth. Not like the man she'd spent a heavenly weekend with just a short time ago. She held off approaching him, any sense of excitement washing away like water down a drain. Instead, she motioned for him to have a seat.

"This is a pleasant surprise."

"Sorry, I'm here without calling first. I hope I'm not interrupting a busy day." Unbuttoning his suit jacket, he sat across the desk from her as Laney took her own seat.

So formal, so...professional. Her senses were

beginning to signal a high alert. "What can I do for you, Gianni?"

"There are things we need to go over, you and I."

"Go over? What kinds of things?"

He took a breath before continuing. "Laney, there was a reason I was here that night. One I didn't fully explain to you."

What in the world was this about? "I don't understand. Why exactly are you here?"

He rubbed his forehead. "I'm here on behalf of Martino Entertainment Enterprises."

Laney had to swallow the brick that had formed at the base of her throat. This was all wrong. "To do what?"

"To make you an offer on your property. We'd like to acquire it as the site of our next casino."

Laney's vision blurred. A dull pounding sounded in her ears. She couldn't have heard him correctly. "Please explain."

"I think you'll be happy with the figure. But of course, we'd be up to negotiate."

Her mouth didn't seem to want to work. How was any of this happening? It had to be some kind of joke. He was teasing her, no doubt. But one look at his face made it clear this was no joking matter.

So that's what that weekend was about. The

only reason he'd said yes to pretending to be her date. Did he think she owed him now?

And to not have told her the truth from the very beginning.

A horrified gasp escaped her lips before she could stop it. She'd asked him to spend the night with her for heaven's sake! What a fool she'd been.

She had to get him out of here before she made an even bigger fool of herself and began to sob. The tears were perilously close, stinging the back of her eyes and clogging her throat.

Standing, she strode to her office door and yanked it open. "This conversation is over, Mr. Martino."

She heard him sigh deeply. Several moments passed when neither one of them moved. Finally, Gianni stood to face her. "Laney, hear me out."

She shook her head. "There's no need. Save your breath. I have no intention of selling. Not to anyone. And especially not to you." She pulled the door wider. "Please leave."

He inhaled deeply. "Laney, listen. I wish things were—"

But she didn't let him finish. There was no point. Everything was so clear. How many times in one lifetime could she let herself be duped like a naive, clueless child?

He was only after her business. The one thing

she was proud of. The one thing she could claim as having done right. Her one true success.

"Please leave now, Mr. Martino."

She'd barely shut the door behind him when the tears began to flow and a sob escaped her lips.

Well, that went well, he thought with bitter sarcasm once he'd left her office.

Gianni entered his car and slammed the door shut so hard the window rattled. Then, for good measure, he pounded the steering wheel hard about half a dozen times with his fists.

It wasn't enough and he wasn't going to be able to get to the gym for another several hours. Laney wasn't even open to the possibility. He'd tried to sound as professional as possible in there, so that he didn't sway her into making a decision based on what they'd shared personally.

But clearly he had hurt her in the process.

How could he have been so foolish? Wanting to get it over with without too many advance questions, he'd simply shown up at her office to tell her all of it in person. It had backfired.

He certainly could have handled the meeting so much better. First, he'd waited too long to tell her the truth, and then he'd botched it royally when he finally had. Now, it was too late to fix things. She would probably never want anything to do with him after this. He wasn't sure what he wanted when it came to Laney Taytum. But he knew with certainty that he would hate to live with the knowledge that she hated him. Though they had no kind of future together, he had to admit he'd grown fond of her. No. It was more than that. He cared for her in a way he hadn't felt for any other woman before in his lifetime. And look at how he'd treated her. It was unconscionable. She'd told him opening that club had been a new beginning for her, after her dreams of becoming a dancer fell through. How could he have forgotten to take that fact into account?

He had to try to do something. Anything.

Part of him wanted to forget what had just happened and just go pummel the punching bag for a good ninety minutes until all the frustration and disgust he felt with himself poured out. But he had too much to do first. He had to go to his father and demand they stop any pursuit of Laney's property. Gianni knew his father wasn't beyond pressure tactics when he was after a business goal, and he never took the first no as a final answer.

That approach was out of the question in this case. He would see to it personally. When it came to Laney, he wouldn't allow it. No matter the cost to himself.

By the time he got to his father's office, his

agitation had only grown. Angelo was there too. That was good. He could make his announcement in one fell swoop—tell them both at once.

His father looked up in surprise when he entered without knocking or so much as announcing his presence. Angelo blinked in question.

"You're back, son. That was quick."

"Hope that means good news," his brother said. "You didn't have to alter too far from our original offer?"

"Not exactly."

His father crossed his arms in front of his chest. "Then why are you back already?"

Gianni loosened his tie and shrugged off his jacket, throwing it behind one of the office chairs. "I've made a decision. You may not like it."

"I already don't," his father responded. Angelo merely raised an eyebrow. When was the last time either of them had directly challenged their father? He couldn't recall. Aside from a rebellious teen tantrum years back, or an inconsequential disagreement about a minor decision, Franco Martino was a hardened man who valued discipline and loyalty, partly because of his background but mostly because of simply who he was and all he'd accomplished. As a result, his sons historically fell in line. Not this time.

"The owner doesn't want to sell. I think we should look elsewhere."

His father rubbed his chin. "I see. Would this happen to be the owner you spent the weekend with? Attending a wedding, if I recall."

"That's not material to this discussion."

Angelo rubbed a hand down his face.

"So you failed to negotiate a deal. Is that correct?" Franco asked.

Gianni made sure to look his father straight in the eye as he answered. He was fully prepared for the dressing down he was sure to receive. It hardly mattered. "That's correct. She doesn't want to sell."

Angelo stepped toward him, his hands up. "Maybe if we just upped the offer."

Gianni shook his head before his brother could even finish. "I won't ask her again."

Angelo dropped his hands as their father responded. "I see."

Gianni somehow doubted that. "We'll have to find another location, Pop."

"That will set us back months."

"So be it."

His father steepled his hands, elbows on his desk. "That's the location I want, son. I thought you understood that."

"Things have changed."

"What kinds of things?" Angelo wanted to know.

Everything had changed. "You'll both just need to take my word for it."

His father eyed him with contemplation. "Your word is gold as far as I'm concerned. Nevertheless. I'd like to try again, see what we have to do to have her accept."

"Then you'll have to do it without me." There it was, he'd thrown down the proverbial gauntlet. And he'd stand firm by it. Franco wasn't used to his authority being questioned in such a blatant manner. But there was a first time for everything.

Ironic, really. How hard had Gianni tried in life to avoid this very thing? How often had he run himself in circles trying to prove himself worthy of being Franco Martino's son? One of his heirs. Given the reality, who Gianni really was—a consequence of a betrayal—this very moment had been one he'd done his best to never experience.

But now, he knew he was doing the right thing. In fact, nothing had ever felt more right. "I refuse to pursue this venue any further."

Angelo's eyebrows went clear up to his hairline, but Gianni could swear he detected a hint of a smile along his lips. It was probably just his imagination.

His father waited several beats before finally answering. "That's very disappointing, son. Shut the door on your way out."

If she didn't finish packing in haste, she was going to miss her flight. But it was hard to pack when one had to consistently stop to throw things at the wall in anger and regret. Not for the first time—okay, maybe for about the hundredth since she'd decided—Laney thought about canceling the trip. After all, never would she have guessed that she'd be taking this journey alone when she first booked it.

But then what? She would just sit here in her apartment during the days wallowing in self-pity and then spend the evenings delivering drinks at the bar while seething with anger. At least being away might take her mind off things for a while. She might even go an hour without thinking of Gianni Martino.

Ha! As if that were likely.

Shaking off the useless thoughts, she made herself focus on the task at hand. Down to the wire, she was just zipping up her carry-on bag when her phone dinged, signaling the arrival of her ride.

No time to second-guess now. Looked like she was on her way to Italy. By herself.

So distracted by her jumbled, angry thoughts, Laney barely noticed about half an hour later when the driver pulled up to the airport departures area and stopped the car. She was right. The timing was definitely close. By the time she reached the gate and boarded, she wouldn't have a minute to spare.

The adrenaline wore off as soon as she sat down in the cabin. The empty seat next to her seemed to mock her. She'd always credited herself as a strong independent woman but right now, all she felt was alone.

And lonely.

Visiting the Amalfi Coast had been a dream of hers for as long as she could remember. Never would she have imagined that she'd be doing so alone. An image of a ruggedly handsome face with dark chocolate eyes and wavy thick hair popped up in her mind and she cursed herself. How could she even be thinking of Gianni Martino at a time like this? She regretted ever running into him that night. She regretted that she hadn't simply swallowed her pride and attended her sister's wedding alone. It would have been so much better than the empty, battered feeling she was wrangling with right now. He was the last person she should wish could accompany her aboard the flight and to Positano, then on to Florence.

But there was no denying, wish it she did. Foolish to the end.

CHAPTER ELEVEN

IT WAS AN official fact. Even on vacation, Laney Taytum was a creature of habit.

By the third day of her dream trip to the coastal tourist town of Positano, Laney had managed to develop something of a routine. She walked the cliffside pathways to get some exercise in the morning. Afternoons were allotted to a leisurely swim in the ocean followed by lounging on the beach with a packed lunch. In the evenings, she perused the many shops for trinkets and souvenirs, then had a quiet dinner in one of the many restaurants or sandwich delis.

It was an utterly charming way to pass the time even if it was rather solitary. Sure, the locals were very friendly. As was the staff at her hotel. She wondered how much of it was the mere characteristic of being a tourist magnet known worldwide. People knew how to treat visitors here.

So she wasn't terribly disturbed the fourth afternoon when a shadow fell over her, blocking the sun as she was sunbathing. Someone she'd met on her escapades so far was stopping to say hi, no doubt.

Until she opened her eyes. Then blinked twice before doing a double take. And then she blinked again.

"Hey, Laney."

Either she was seeing things, things she wanted to see, or Gianni Martino was standing over her on the beach. Half a world away from where she'd last seen him.

This couldn't be real. Sitting up, Laney blocked the sun glare with her hand, the hand that was shaking just a tad less than the other. Somehow, she got her mouth to work. "Tell me something. Do you happen to have a twin who lives in Boston?" She couldn't even tell for sure if she was joking.

He laughed and the sound of it gave it away. She'd recognize that laugh anywhere. Scrambling to her feet, "Gianni? What in the world—"

"Surprised to see me?"

If that weren't the understatement of the decade. Or the century.

This had to be some kind of weird coincidence. He'd said he had family here nearby. Maybe some kind of emergency had come up with one of his relatives. But that didn't explain his presence here, on the beach. Where he'd found her. Coincidence surely couldn't go that far. "What are you doing here?"

"I remembered which hotel you said you were staying in. This is the closest beach, so I took a chance."

"Not that. I mean, what are you doing here? In Italy?"

"I couldn't leave things the way they were between us. The truth is, I owe you an apology."

She had to give her head a shake to chase away the fog of confusion. "And you decided to fly across the world to do it."

He had the gall to wink at her, just like that first night, making her heart tug just a tad in her chest and she chastised herself silently for it. She would *not* fall for his charm that easily again. She'd only laid eyes on him again for about two minutes, for heaven's sake. "You couldn't have just called or something?"

He shrugged sheepishly. "It was a pretty big apology. Some things are worth a bit of effort or a long flight across the ocean."

"Yeah. I'd say."

He stepped closer to her. That spicy masculine aftershave she'd gotten so fond of back in Boston drifted on the ocean breeze and made her shudder. How inconvenient that she was still so attracted to this man.

But first things first. "Go on, then. Let's hear this apology you flew to Italy to give."

He rubbed his chin. "I should have been up-front with you from the get-go. I have no excuse. It's just that after we met, one thing led to another, and there never seemed to be a good time. Things just sort of snowballed. I'm usually in better control of my variables than that. I'm sorry, Laney. More than you could know."

Wow. Sounded as if he'd given this some thought. He had to be sincere. He'd gone through an awful lot of trouble to deliver his sorry in person. But she was still nursing her wounds. Transatlantic flight or not. What he'd done back in Boston wasn't insignificant.

She crossed her arms. "What about my club? I take it your family is still after it?"

"I confess that's true. They have their eyes on it, given it's prime real estate near the water and its proximity to the heart of the city. Just keep turning them down."

She squinted at him. "Them?"

He swallowed and nodded. "I've removed myself from the project. And I'll do everything I can to try to get them to look elsewhere. Before getting to know you, I hadn't realized how much the place meant to you. That's not an excuse, I know."

"It's a start."

"I'd like to make it all up to you. If you'll let me."

Her logical mind screamed that she should walk away now. Tell him he shouldn't have bothered coming all this way. But a small yet stronger voice, the one that seemed to always get her in trouble, had other plans in mind. Her curiosity got the better of her.

"How exactly?" She couldn't begin to guess what the answer to that question may be.

"Well, it occurred to me how serendipitous it is that you happened to be traveling to Positano, given how well I know the city. And given the fact that I have family here."

"So?"

"So there has to be some kind of kismet there, wouldn't you say?"

What exactly was he getting at? "You need to spell out for me exactly what you have in mind, Gianni. I'm not in the mood for guessing games."

He nodded once. "Fair enough. Like I said, I know the area really well. And you don't. Let me play at tour guide. Show you a side of Positano only a local would know."

"Tour guide?"

He motioned around him. "This city is like no other. I can make it so that you have memories to last you a lifetime. It's the least I can do to begin to make amends."

"You want to show me around Positano as a way to redeem yourself."

He visibly winced. "In a nutshell. If you say no, I'll walk off this beach and you'll never hear from me again. If that's what you want."

"Huh." It was the only word she could come up with. Her mind was blank. If someone had told her during the flight here that she'd be faced with such a decision on her fourth day of the trip, she would have laughed, then asked which bridge they were selling.

She started to say no. But there was that pestering, obnoxious voice again that always got her into trouble. The voice that seemed to forget all the times she'd been naively foolish enough to think she could have something simply because she wanted it so badly. She started packing up her things, just to stall.

"I think I've had enough sun. I'm going to head back to the hotel."

He nodded, and tried to help her gather her towel before she pushed his hand away. "Can I walk you back to your room?"

Straightening, she studied his face. Those eyes that she'd lost herself in that one fateful weekend. The smile that charmed the socks off her the first time she'd seen it.

She just couldn't do it. She couldn't bring herself to turn him down flat, though she knew it was the only right thing to do.

"I'll have to think about your offer," she said over her shoulder as she walked away.

"You know how to get a hold of me," he said behind her.

She didn't dare look back, too tempted to change her mind and say yes then and there.

Positano certainly seemed to be the land of lovers.

Laney sat down at the solitary corner table at the bistro a member of the hotel staff had recommended to her. All the center tables were full. Most of them occupied by couples, many of whom were holding hands or sharing bites of each other's food. One handsome gentleman was actually spoon-feeding his companion, landing a kiss occasionally between bites. An older couple, one table over from them, raised their wineglasses in a toast.

Laney made herself look away from the romantic scenes and focused on the menu instead. Without pulling out her phone and calling up the translation app, she could only make out a couple of items. One particular dish jumped out at her. Gnocchi.

She certainly knew that one.

Images of the night in Gianni's apartment as he cooked for her flooded her mind. He'd been so charming that night, so attractive in his chef's apron. A warm current ran up her spine as she remembered the way he'd stood behind her and held her arm to show her how to roll the potato dough. A current of ire bolted through her center suddenly. He could have told her then, that very night. Instead, he'd let her continue to think their paths had simply crossed coincidentally. He'd kept her in the dark until it was too late and she'd grown to care for him.

But he was looking to make it up to her now. Could she really take him up on it? He was here, merely miles away in the same town. She would have never guessed when she'd arrived in Italy three days ago that he might follow her. Hard to deny the fact that she felt rather touched that he'd done so.

Was she actually considering accepting his offer to show her around?

She mentally ran through the pros and cons. Yes, she was still angry. And hurt. But she could be smarter about their relationship now. Part of the reason his admission had hit her so hard was that she'd begun developing feelings for him. She had no such delusions about doing so now.

Nothing said spending time with him had to have any underlying emotional undertones. Not if she made sure to keep her emotions in check this time.

As long as she made clear that the arrangement was nothing more than that. She'd let him accompany her through Positano, let him show her the sights he knew so well. And at the end of the day, they'd go to their separate rooms.

She wouldn't soon forget what he'd done. The way he'd misled her. But the man had traveled across the world in an attempt to make amends. Would it be so bad to take him up on it? Especially if it meant she wouldn't have to spend the rest of the week all by herself. The solitary tourist thing was getting a little old.

Agreeing to his offer made logical sense, as well. Many of the excursions she'd signed up for and the meals that were part of the package deal were included for two individuals. Though money was the least of her worries at the moment, it was something to consider.

"Scusi?" The server interrupted her thoughts. "You are expecting someone, *si*?" he asked in broken English, taking away the other menu that sat in a center holder.

She shook her head in answer. No, tonight she wasn't expecting anyone else to join her. She'd spend yet another evening by herself. But that didn't have to be the case going forward.

As Gianni had said, the decision was completely up to her.

* * *

"Hiking? We're going hiking?"

She wasn't expecting Gianni's first outing for her as a tour guide to be quite so physical. Laney looked down at her open-toed soft leather sandals and her butter-beige newly untagged capri pants. He'd told her to meet him for breakfast at the lobby restaurant of her hotel to discuss what he had planned. Clearly, she should have asked first about proper attire for their day trip.

Gianni followed the direction of her gaze. "Yeah, you might want to run back upstairs and change into more rugged shoes."

"The most rugged pair I brought with me are sneakers."

"That should work," he reassured her.

Now that she thought about it, she remembered reading about one of Positano's more famous, if not less glamorous, attractions in a travel agency brochure. A hiking trail along the cliffside. Not usually a hiker type, she hadn't given it much thought. Gianni was telling her it was not to be missed. Still, she had reservations.

Gianni had already ordered and had the breakfast waiting for her when she'd come downstairs. She found herself ridiculously grateful that the food was there and ready, particularly the coffee. Laney took a sip of her strong espresso and tore off a piece of the brioche, then popped it into her mouth. "Just how strenuous is this going to be?" she asked.

"You dance every night to bouncy pop songs and carry heavy trays laden with bottles and cocktails. I think you can handle it."

Dancing and delivering drinks used entirely different muscles and skills than the ones required to ascend mountainside cliffs. Nevertheless, she ran upstairs quickly to change into her athletic shoes and a pair of denim shorts while Gianni waited.

When she arrived back down at the lobby, Gianni was loading up the backpack he'd brought with snacks and bottles of water.

"I'm ready," she told him. Or as ready as she was ever going to be. Growing up in New England, she'd visited more than her fair share of mountains and thought herself a skilled and experienced skier. But none of those mountains could be considered anything near cliff-like.

She hoped Gianni knew what he was doing here.

In moments, they were boarding a late-model SUV helmed by a uniformed driver.

"We'll get dropped off at Agerola. And the path will bring us back to Nocelle," Gianni explained as she buckled herself in the back seat next to him. The way he pronounced the names of the cities in a fluid Italian accent sounded alluring and exotic. "Should take about an hour or so to drive there."

"Nocelle?"

"It's the cliffside village right above Positano." He pointed up toward the sky. "We'll be over a thousand or so feet above where we started from."

Well, that implied there was a piece of the overall puzzle missing. "And how do we get down, then?"

"That's the best part." The smile he gave her sent a small shiver down her spine. She wanted to pretend it was due to the adventure ahead of them and nothing more.

"How so?"

"We go down the stairs."

She felt her jaw drop as she took in what he said. "Over a thousand feet of stairs."

"Can you handle it?"

"I'm not sure. That's a lot of steps."

"About fifteen hundred or so."

They were driving around tight roads through commercial shops and street-side vendors. A quaint scene of seaside life in Italy she probably would have enjoyed more if she wasn't worrying about how her legs would handle a thousand plus number of steps after hiking a trail for a couple of hours.

"Come on," Gianni said. "You're pretty fit. You lead weekly fitness classes. The way you carry all those cocktails and bottles. And those fitness classes you teach." He did a move as he performed small double kicks behind the seat in what she assumed was meant to imitate an aerobic workout step. A bubble of laughter escaped her lips.

"That's not quite the same as jumping down miles worth of steps, is it?"

He shrugged. "At least I'm no making you go up the steps. Why I hired a car to get us up there."

She shuddered at the thought. "Well, thank you for that."

"You'll have fun, I promise," he said as he placed his hand on her thigh above her knee. She couldn't even help the images that immediately flooded her mind at his touch. Memories of their one night together after the wedding reception.

Different time. Different place.

She'd learned her lesson when it came to this man. No, she was simply enjoying his company as a friend who happened to be familiar with the foreign city she was visiting. He was helping her to make the most of this trip. There absolutely could not be a replay of the events that had led them into each other's arms. She simply didn't have it in her to deal with the emotional fallout.

As if sensing her thoughts, Gianni quickly removed his hand. He pointed to a spot outside her passenger-side window. "That place has the best gelato this side of the ocean. Remind me to have us stop there at some point."

See, his comment was further cementing her point. She would have had no idea where to go to get the best gelato. Heck, it might not have even occurred to her that she wanted any. And she might have missed going on this hiking path altogether if it weren't for Gianni.

Suddenly, she felt better about her decision to take him up on being her companion for the next couple of days or so. Then she'd be off to Florence for the next adventure. He hadn't offered to accompany her there, and she wouldn't ask him to. He was only here in Positano because he could helpfully show her around the area.

A pang of regret tugged at her chest that she'd be alone once again after she got to Florence. But she shook it off. One step at a time. Starting with the ones that would follow their massive hike.

Pretty soon the shops and vendor carts gave way to a narrow stone-lined path surrounded by the greenest shrubbery she'd ever seen.

"How long will we be hiking?"

Gianni gave a small shrug. "Depends how often we stop. You brought your camera like I asked?"

She nodded in answer.

"Trust me, you'll want to pause several times to take photos. You're not going to believe the visionary treat that's in store for you."

All right. He had her curiosity piqued. "There's a reason it's called Il Sentiero degli Dei."

"What's that mean?"

"The Path of the Gods."

So celestial. And a little under an hour later, Laney was well on the way to fully grasping exactly why the hiking path had such a divine name. View after view was more breathtaking than the last. She'd taken countless photos. The crystal blue ocean beneath them reminded her of the finest turquoise jewelry, the greenery a color of rich jade she'd never seen before.

A visual buffet of magnificence that had her gasping with wonder as they reached each new vantage point. By the time they reached the massive array of steps over two hours later, she was panting and her midsection felt tight and fluttery.

Gianni noticed. "Are you all right?" He handed her a bottle of water.

She nodded. "All the excitement. Plus, I'm famished. Those granola bars only did so much to tide me over." Funny, now that she thought about it, she realized she'd been hungrier on this trip than she could ever remember being. Waiting for the next mealtime had proven impossible most days, and she'd found herself down in the hotel concierge floor to nab a bite, or stopping in a shop along her way to the beach. Who knew going on a bucket-list trip would so arouse a girl's appetite?

Gianni studied her with concern for a beat, then hoisted his backpack. "Then let's get down these steps posthaste. We'll get you an authentic Italian meal you won't soon forget."

Gianni could barely contain his amusement when he led Laney to the front door of a charming two-story box building, rather than to the entrance of a bistro like she'd no doubt been expecting.

"Where are we?" she asked, as he led her up the steps and knocked on the door. "Did you need to run an errand or something?"

Her voice was on the verge of snappy and she looked mildly annoyed. Like his younger clients at the gym would call it, she was "hangry." He had to get some food in her and soon. This was just the place. "I promised you an authentic Positano meal like no other."

"But this is clearly someone's house," she protested while the sound of footsteps could be heard behind the door.

"Trust me."

The door swung open at that moment and the familiar matronly face of his favorite *zia* beamed at them from across the threshold.

"Gianni! *Mi bambino. Bene! Bene!*"

She stepped out onto the porch and enveloped

him in a tight affectionate hug. When she finally let go, she turned her attention to Laney who looked rather shell-shocked. Her expression only grew in surprise when Zia Rosa took her by the arm and led her inside behind her.

"Come in…come in," she said in perfect English, albeit with a thick Italian accent. "We were expecting you tomorrow."

"Change in plans," Gianni answered. "Hope that's okay."

"Yeah, it's okay. You are welcome here any time of day whenever you wish."

He knew that, of course. Laney didn't look convinced, however. He made brief introductions, explaining to Laney exactly where they were and who was leading her to a center table and sitting her down on one of the chairs.

"Dinner won't be for another couple of hours," his aunt announced. "But let me get you some bruschetta while you wait. And there's some soup left from lunch. You are both hungry, yes?"

"Yes. But we don't want to impose, Signora Rosa." She stopped long enough to send him a fierce glare across the table as he took his own seat. "I had no idea we were coming. Unannounced, no less."

His *zia* scoffed, setting a steaming bowl of minestrone and a plate of fragrant bruschetta in front of them both. "Nonsense. Family needs no announcement."

"Rosa spent years studying international affairs in London," Gianni explained. "Her English is more proper than mine."

"I can see that." Laney seemed to have suddenly lost her earlier hesitancy, once the soup and veggie-loaded tray of bread were placed in front of her. His aunt's warmth and hospitality had surely helped, as well.

Rosa turned to retrieve more bread from the pantry. Laney leaned over the table as soon as she left the room.

"We shouldn't have come unannounced, Gianni."

He waved away the comment. "Stop worrying about it. Italy isn't like the States. Friends and family often just show up. Particularly family that happens to be visiting from half a world away."

Her eyebrows drew together, making it rather clear she didn't quite believe him. "What if she was out? Or if it was a bad time?"

He shrugged. "If it happens to be an inconvenient time, the visitor is just told so. And they wander off to come back and visit another day."

Laney leaned back against her chair. "Huh. You're right. That's completely different from how things are in the States. It's definitely different from the way I grew up."

Yeah, he'd gotten the impression even before her sister's wedding that her family was rather keen on formality and proper decorum. Rules in general.

"Yeah, and there's always food," he answered, helping himself to more. Particularly at an older aunt's house, regardless of the time of day.

Good thing too. He could practically hear Laney's stomach grumbling from three feet away.

She looked right here, at his aunt's small wooden table in her cozy kitchen. As if she belonged. And it felt right, to have her in this house, with him. As if she belonged by his side.

There was no doubt Zia Rosa had already taken a liking to her. He would have gotten some kind of stink-eye look by now if that weren't the case.

Still, he couldn't help but notice the slight dark circles under Laney's eyes, the tight set of her mouth. The way she still hadn't seemed to fully catch her breath. She looked fatigued, weary. He would have to make sure to get her back to her hotel room early so she could rest.

Their long hike and the subsequent trek down the Nocelle stairs had worn her down more than he would have expected.

Just went to show, even when his heart was in the right place, he couldn't seem to do right by Laney Taytum.

CHAPTER TWELVE

THREE HOURS LATER, after yet another scrumptious meal of seafood and homemade pasta, Gianni took her upstairs to sit on the balcony. Between the view of the ocean in the distance as the sun set and the quaint scenes of walkers and playing children in the street below, Laney felt as if she could be sitting in a painting. Straight out of the Italian Renaissance.

Just more affirmation that besides the awkwardness of the situation, she had made the right decision about Gianni accompanying her. By contrast, if she hadn't taken him up on his offer, she'd be alone in her hotel room right now with a paperback or trying to discern the Italian on some random television show.

Heavens, she felt tired though. More so than she'd felt in as long a time as she could remember. Her days back home were rather physical, so it was somewhat surprising that she was feeling so bone-deep exhausted.

"Did we over do it today?" Gianni asked next

to her, tilting his chair back on its two back legs, reading her thoughts. But then, he seemed to have a knack for doing that. It hardly even surprised her anymore.

"So I look as exhausted as I feel, then?"

"You always look beautiful, Laney."

Good thing the sun was setting, hopefully the shadows would prevent him from noticing the slight flush that instantly rushed to her cheeks at the compliment.

"But you do look rather tired," he added. "Sorry if the hike was too much."

She shook her head, wondering how he was managing to not topple backward as far as that chair was tilted. "Probably still some jet lag lingering on top of the exertion of the hike."

He looked concerned enough that she wanted to change the subject. "Your aunt is a lovely woman," she told him. "And quite a cook," she added, rubbing her belly. "I may never enjoy another meal again after that work of art she set in front of us."

"She is at that. It's too bad my cousin is away on business. You would have liked him. He's quite a character."

"Then it must be a family trait. Something in the genes."

She was certain she didn't imagine the slight wince and the sudden lift of his shoulders.

“Aunt Rosa is my father’s sister,” he said, as if that explained anything.

“I’m guessing you think you take after your mother’s side of the family more.”

The clang of metal hitting the wooden balcony floor rang through the air as he straightened the chair finally to sit on all four legs.

“You could say that.” He stood suddenly. “I’ll be right back.”

When he returned about a minute later, he held a frosty tall bottle full of bright yellow liquid, along with two bottles of water and a couple of glasses.

“Limoncello,” he declared, holding up the bottle. “Homemade by said cousin you have the misfortune of not being able to meet this visit.”

As refreshing as the drink sounded, alcohol was definitely not what she wanted or needed at the moment. She could barely keep her eyes open as it was. But the sweaty bottle of water was practically calling to her.

“Maybe later. I will take the water from you though.”

“Are you sure? This stuff is made from the ripest lemons grown only in this part of the world.”

She absolutely was. “Just the water for now, please.”

He tossed it to her with a shrug. “Suit yourself.”

Tiny effervescent bubbles floated in the air as he poured himself the limoncello. The aroma tickled her nose and she imagined herself walking through a fruitful citrus garden. She would have to make a note to add a limoncello-based drink at the club when she returned to Boston.

Gianni seemed to have gone silent, sipping his drink slowly and staring at the ocean in the distance. The water was growing a darker, deeper shade of blue as the sun lowered farther into the horizon.

Taking a long drink of her water, she tried to keep the conversation going. "So, tell me about this cousin of yours. He's clearly some kind of drink master."

Gianni scoffed, didn't turn to her as he answered. "He's not really my cousin."

"He's not?"

"No. And Aunt Rosa's not really my aunt. And my father is definitely not—" He cut off the words, took another drink instead. This time it was way more than a sip.

Laney gave a shake of her head. Obviously, she was missing something.

He made the universal sign of sealed lips in a clearly mocking gesture. "But don't tell anyone. No one can talk about it. Even though everyone knows."

Understanding began to dawn. "Oh, do you

mean you were adopted?" It was the only explanation that made sense of what he was saying.

"Not quite. I was the product of an extramarital affair."

Laney bit down on her gasp of surprise. Just barely. She could hardly find the words to respond. Exactly what did one say to such an admission?

Several beats of awkward silence ensued until she finally broke it with the truth. "I don't know what to say, Gianni. Other than that, from what I can see, you were born into and grew up in a loving family."

His fingers had tightened on the glass he held. She worried it might shatter in his hand. "That's the absolute truth. Except for one small yet significant detail."

"What's that?"

"The only reason my father calls me his son is because he'd never admit anyone on earth would have the audacity to betray him. Especially not the woman he fell in love with and made his wife."

Gianni couldn't believe what he'd just shared with her.

He couldn't remember the last time he'd talked about his heritage. If ever.

He turned to her now in the ever-growing darkness, fully prepared to see the pity on her lovely face. After all, how would someone like Laney Taytum, with her pedigree of perfect professionals ever understand what he'd just admitted.

But the expression Laney wore was one of clear concern. He wasn't sure that was much better.

"How did you find out?" she asked.

He let out a deep breath. "I can hardly remember. During one of our Italy visits when a distant uncle didn't realize I was rather fluent in Italian. I was fairly young, but not too young to understand what had just been revealed." There'd been no point in anyone denying it wasn't true. His mom had taken off one day, leaving nothing but a note behind that she'd found someone else. Gianni had never been told all the details, but something had made her return to Franco even as she carried another man's child.

"Everyone just sort of ignored it," he told Laney. "And I was just a kid. So I followed along."

"And you've kept it to yourself? All these years?"

"Not really. After college, I visited Aunt Rosa. She was the one person who I knew wouldn't lie to me. She confirmed my suspicions in not so many words."

Laney reached over the arm of her chair to rub the top of his hand. A small gesture, but one he found oddly soothing. "She clearly loves you,

Gianni. I can tell just from these past few hours that she loves you deeply. I have three aunts. None of which I can say I'm particularly close to." She pointed back toward the house. "Not like what I witnessed in that house between you and that lady in there."

Huh. Maybe she did understand, after all. Who would have thought?

"Did you ever approach your mother for answers?"

He released a deep sigh. "I tried. My mother wouldn't even breach the subject.

"And you stopped bringing it up."

He shrugged. "What choice did I have? What would have been the point in confronting anyone?"

"How brave of you."

He had to chuckle at that. "How in the world is any of that being brave?"

Her hand tightened around his. "It is. You never hurt either one of your parents by confronting them. You even work for your father."

That last part was almost certainly about to change but she didn't need to know all that. He'd divulged enough to her already.

More than enough.

"We should probably drop it," he said, tilting his head in the direction of the house. "I don't want Zia to hear any of this conversation."

"Of course," she said, immediately dropping his hand. Gianni felt the loss of her touch right down in his center.

He lifted his glass. "Here's to family," he said in a toast that was meant to be ironic. "And to this gorgeous sunset."

Laney took the cue and remained silent for several minutes. For a good part of the hour, they simply sat and admired the changing colors of the sky and the ocean below it. Eventually, the passersby in the street below slowed to a trickle. The sound of children kicking around a ball had already ceased.

It was probably time to call it a night and get Laney back to her hotel. But when he turned to tell her so, he stopped short. She had her arms folded in front of her. Her chest rose and fell in a steady, slow rhythm. Her head lay tilted on her shoulder.

She was sound asleep.

With a sigh, he stood and went to her, then gently lifted her out of the chair, taking care not to wake her. She really had looked tired. The best thing for her now was just to get some rest. Rosa had a spare bedroom she usually kept clean and ready given all the various visitors she was accustomed to. And he certainly wasn't any stranger to crashing on a couch now and again. He knew his aunt wouldn't mind the company.

Walking back into the house, he made his way toward the hallway and back to the spare room. He set Laney down on the spare bed, and threw one of Zia Rosa's hand-crocheted covers over her.

For one long moment, he simply let himself indulge by watching her. They'd known each other only a short time but had gone through quite a bit together already. No wonder he'd felt at ease enough to share his family's deep-seated secret with her. Something about her had called to him from the moment he'd laid eyes on her.

Too bad it couldn't go anywhere. She was the first woman to have him even so much as reconsider his stance about a long-term relationship. Laney Taytum had him thinking all sorts of scenarios he would have previously never considered for himself. But it was all just wishful thinking. They were from completely different worlds. She came from a strong lineage of overachievers and knew exactly who she was. While he was a man who didn't even rightfully belong in his family and had no idea who'd sired him. She was much too far out of his league.

Finally, he turned to leave, taking care to step softly over the creak he knew was there on the wooden floor under the plush rug.

He was about to shut the door behind him when he heard her low voice in the darkness.

"Please stay."

He hesitated for just the briefest second. But then resigned himself. He wouldn't be able to turn her down. Pulling off his T-shirt, he slipped under the blanket and took her in his arms.

He couldn't even explain what happened next. He meant to give her just a small quick peck on the cheek as a good-night. But she turned her head at just the right moment. Or maybe it was the wrong moment. But his lips found hers. Then he was tasting her mouth, a low groan rumbling in her throat. Her arms wrapped around him, her chest tight against his own. He simply savored the taste of her, blanketed in the warmth of her body. Gentle yet untamed. Full of yearning. He might not ever get enough.

It was over all too soon. Gianni didn't even know which one of them pulled away first. Both of them remained silent for several beats, the kiss hanging heavy in the air between them. Finally, Laney released a deep sigh, whether from weariness or regret for the unplanned kiss, he didn't know and wasn't sure he wanted to find out. But she didn't ask him to leave. So he simply held her as she fell asleep, until the morning light woke them both.

So this was goodbye. Gianni cursed under his breath and tried not think about their kiss that night. He'd been a fool for thinking even for a moment that it might have meant anything more than a temporary lapse in judgement. Laney was leaving for Florence. And he would just have to find a way to forget about her.

Easier said than done.

Now, Gianni watched Laney's retreating back as she made her way down the platform at the Nocera Inferiore train station, her dark curls bouncing along her shoulders. Rushing because she was convinced she was late.

On her way to sunny Florence.

Amazing just how fast three days had gone by. During his weaker moments over those days, he'd been tempted to offer to travel there with her. Luckily, those temptations passed quickly. For it was better this way, better to make a clean break. He hadn't spent much time in Florence, thus had no excuse to accompany her as any kind of guide or expert.

He would be of no use to her. Moot point. Not like she'd asked him to accompany her.

Laney Taytum was off on her next adventure. An adventure that had no room for him. He'd set her up to meet one of his distant cousins, just so she wasn't alone when she first arrived. His part in her travels was over. As was any part he had in her life. Anyway, he had to get back to the States. So much there needed to be attended to.

For one, he had to figure out a way to buy out his share of Martino Entertainment Enterprises in case he was no longer wanted as part of the company. His father had been eerily quiet since Gianni had so openly defied him about pursuing Laney's club. The gym-and-fitness arm was his brainchild. He'd developed and grown that piece and had no intention of letting it go easy.

Starting over with a competing business was always an option but one he'd rather avoid. He just had to get the old man to agree. He almost chuckled out loud. Piece of cake. Trying to convince that man of anything once he made up his mind was like putting out a four-alarm fire by blowing on it.

So much of Gianni's professional life was up in the air at the moment. Yet another reason he had to forget Laney Taytum existed. Maybe they'd run into each other on the streets of Boston. Who knew? Perhaps next time he saw her, she'd be accompanied by the man she was meant to be with. Someone more appropriate, who would fit better in her world and with her family.

A rage of emotion he refused to acknowledge as jealousy rushed through his midsection at the thought before he shoved it aside. Any regret he may feel was his burden to bear.

Still, he couldn't help the deep longing he felt when she turned back to wave at him one more time, then disappeared from his sight completely. That was it, then. No more looking back for either of them. He'd check with his relative to make sure she arrived in Florence safely and that she was settled in well at her next hotel. His cousin Zara had promised to set her up with a reputable tour company who would make sure she was well taken care of.

He hoped she had the time of her life. And he hoped life for her afterward continued to be adventurous and full of happiness. It was no less than what she deserved.

He really was a lovely specimen. The perfect man, actually. Every muscle chiseled and perfect. His tall imposing frame sent a shiver of excitement up her spine. How long had Laney waited for this moment? Probably her whole life.

Yep, the statue of David was everything she had expected and more.

Just looking at him took her breath away. That had to be the reason for the quaking in her stomach. Pure adrenaline begotten by finally setting her eyes on one of the world's greatest artistic creations. Only, it didn't explain the mild nausea that had plagued her since boarding the train from the Amalfi Coast. She pushed back the memories that threatened to assault her mind as she thought about her time there. Gianni hadn't asked her to stay, not even for another day or so. Nor had he offered to travel with her to Florence. How foolish of her to think even for a moment that he might. He'd felt bad about what had transpired between them in Boston and he'd made up for his mistake by playing tour guide in Positano. Now that his conscience was clear, he was moving on.

Enough. Laney had to move on too. She couldn't think about Gianni Martino. She was here on the second part of her bucket-list trip, darn it. And she was going to make the most of her time here. Starting with an attempt to sketch the marvelous work of art that stood before her now. Drawing and painting weren't exactly her strongest creative skills, but she thought she had more talent than what was currently being shown. It seemed to be taking a lot of effort to drag the pencil across the page to form any semblance of a depiction of the statue.

Maybe she should have had more for breakfast. Being in Italy certainly made her ravenous.

Visiting the statue first clearly wasn't a good idea. She should have started with the paintings farther down the hall. The *Madonna with Child* would no doubt be breathtaking.

Child. A nagging suspicion crawled into the back of her mind and she almost swatted the thought away. But it persisted.

It couldn't be.

The sketch pad fell out of her hands. Slowly standing up, she felt the blood rush to her limbs. Several deep, even breaths didn't do much to settle her nerves.

Could this really be happening? The constant hunger, the fatigue, the mild nausea that hit her without warning. All the clues of the past few weeks started coming together. What if her suspicions were founded? What then? It was too much to think about.

Her sketching was going to have to wait. Right now, she had to get back to the hotel and ask about the nearest pharmacy or medical center. Time seemed to flow into another dimension as she slowly made her way out of the museum. Disoriented and scared, she turned the wrong way before fixing her mistake and turning in the right direction.

An hour later, she had her answer. Laney couldn't seem to move, blindly staring out the window at the piazza outside. Her mind was a complete scramble. She had bought two tests just to be sure. Both results were the same. She shuddered at the thought of telling her parents. But she would do so and she would make sure everything that came from now on would be her decision and hers alone. She had more than herself to think about now.

And Gianni. Her heart did a little somersault in her chest as she thought of how she would tell him. One of the first things he'd announced about himself was just how much he wasn't interested in things like getting married or having a family.

She was all alone in this. Same as ever.

CHAPTER THIRTEEN

SHE REHEARSED HOW her end of the conversation might go one more time before picking up her cell phone. Laney had started the practice during her long trip back to Boston. Somehow, all the rehearsing didn't seem to be making it any easier. With a frustrated huff, she threw her phone back down on the sofa. She couldn't do it, couldn't sum up the courage.

How in the world was she going to tell Gianni that she was pregnant with his baby? Would he blame her?

She could only hope he'd be a better man than that.

There was a very real possibility he'd want nothing to do with her when she told him. Or their child. She would just have to accept that and learn to live with it somehow. Though the thought that Gianni would turn his back on her when she was the mother of his child sliced her with a searing hurt.

Only one way to find out. This was going to

be the most important and probably the most nerve-racking phone call she'd ever have to make. And she absolutely couldn't put it off any longer. She'd been back in the States three days already.

To think, she'd almost deleted his number from her phone. After he'd dropped her off at the train station and said goodbye as if they were never meant to see each other again, it had seemed the most prudent thing to do. Why in the world would it have occurred to her that she'd need to call that number in a few days? They'd been careful. Or so she'd thought.

Her hand shook as she picked the phone up and called up his contact info. Without giving herself another chance to chicken out, she hit the dial icon. And puffed out a sigh in frustration as soon as it went through.

Voice mail.

Or maybe it was a sigh of relief. She hardly knew her right from her left at the moment. She hadn't even considered she'd get his voice mail. Hormones must be scrambling her brain, given that the possibility hadn't even occurred to her during all those rehearsals she'd gone over in her mind. She practically flung the phone across the room over onto the love seat.

It rang the second it landed on the cushion. She knew without looking that it had to be him, though it was the standard ringtone. Walking with heavy steps to retrieve it, she clicked on the call without giving herself a chance to chicken out. But no words would come out of her mouth.

"Laney? Is that you?" His voice washed over her like the smoothest waterfall. It had only been a few days since she'd seen him, but it seemed so much longer. A lot had happened.

She'd missed him.

"Laney? Did you just call me?" he asked.

For an insane moment, she thought about lying that it had been a pocket dial. But that would just be putting off the inevitable. She forced her mouth to work. "Yes, it's me. Hello, Gianni."

"Hello. Are you calling from Florence? Is everything okay?"

"Yes. I mean, no." Oh, Lord. This call was going so poorly. "I mean I'm calling from Boston. Just decided to cut the trip short a little bit."

I don't know if everything is okay.

"Oh. I see. Weren't you enjoying your trip?"

Not after we parted, she almost said out loud before she caught herself. "Something came up. Something you should know about. It's why I'm calling. Otherwise, I wouldn't have bothered you."

Nothing but silence came through the tiny speaker for several beats. Finally, he spoke. "Sounds serious. Maybe you should just tell me."

"Well, you might want to sit down. If you're standing, that is." Wow. She really wasn't handling this well at all.

"Laney, tell me, sweetheart."

"Well, it just so happens, that I'm pregnant," she blurted out, just like ripping off the proverbial bandage. An adequate analogy, given the pain she was experiencing. "I found out in Florence."

She heard him suck in a breath. "Our weekend in Boston?" he asked.

"Yes. It had to be."

"Okay. I see."

"I thought you should know."

"And you're absolutely certain?"

What a question. She wouldn't be calling him otherwise. This wasn't the kind of news a woman broke on a hunch or guess, after all. "I took two different tests in Italy. Then confirmed with my doctor once I arrived back in the States."

"Guess that settles it. Are you feeling well?"

"Yes. For the most part." Physically, she was hanging in there. Her emotional state was another matter entirely. "Just hungry a lot. You know what they say about eating for two." She chuckled at her own rather lame attempt at lightening the moment.

"Well, uh, thank you. For letting me know." He paused for what had to be a second. But on her end, it may as well have been a lifetime.

"Uh, you're welcome?" For the life of her, she couldn't come up with anything else to say. She'd been right. This really was the most awkward phone call she'd ever made.

"But I thought we were—"

She cut him off. "Yeah. I did too. I guess not enough."

"Huh. Okay. I see."

He really had to stop repeating that or she was going to lose her mind completely. Only what he said right after was even worse.

"Yeah. So, listen, can I call you back?"

"Call me back?"

"Uh-huh. I'm actually in the middle of a rather important meeting."

A meeting? He wanted to interrupt this earth-shattering news she was delivering because of a business meeting? "Oh. Of course. Sorry." Why in the world was she apologizing? "For interrupting the meeting, I mean."

"Okay. I see."

Laney rolled her eyes. He was clearly at a loss for words. Or maybe he was just really concerned that he was missing his important meeting.

It hardly mattered. She'd delivered the news. The rest was up to him, the ball completely in his court.

"I'll let you get back to it, then," she told him, clicking off the call without saying goodbye.

Tears stung the back of her eyes as she sank down into the floor. His reaction was one she would have never guessed. She'd had less business-sounding calls with her wine supplier.

She was a fool to have expected any different.

Gianni slipped the phone back into his pocket and braced himself against the wall with one arm. Laney's phone call seemed like some kind of daydream. As if he'd just made it up.

But it was all too real, he knew. A baby. His baby.

The new reality was going to take some time for him to process. The truth was, he hadn't seen this coming by a light-year. He knew he could have handled the call better than he had. He'd just been so shocked by the news. So he'd tried to be very careful with his words, saying less for fear of saying the wrong thing. Perhaps he'd been a bit too straightforward and narrow with his response. But that was better than the alternative. Hurting her somehow or making a statement she didn't agree with.

For all he knew, she might not even want him in this child's life. That thought felt like a slice across his midsection. If that were the case, he'd have to do all he could to convince her otherwise. He couldn't live with himself if his reality was to live his life as an absentee father. Or worse, if he were made to simply stand back and let another man raise his son or daughter.

But he was getting way ahead of himself. First, he had to let it all fully sink in. And he had to check in on Laney as soon as was feasible.

His accountant stepped out into the hallway. "Mr. Martino? Has something come up? Did you want to reschedule?"

Gianni didn't even realize how long he'd been standing out there. It could have been an hour or merely a few minutes. He just remembered jumping out of his chair and running out of the room when he'd realized he'd missed Laney's call. "No. I don't want to reschedule. In fact, there's an entirely different matter we need to discuss."

The man lifted an eyebrow in question.

"On top of the financial documents to present to my father for a purchase offer, I'd like to establish a few trust and college funds with investment to begin immediately."

His accountant didn't bother to question him, simply motioned for him to step back into the room. Good thing too—Gianni wasn't sure how he would even try to explain the additional request that seemed to have come out of nowhere.

Besides, his finance man wasn't the first person he intended to announce the fact that he was going to be a father. The words echoed around in his head, like musical notes ricocheting off the chambers of his mind.

He was going to be a father.

Two and a half hours later, as he arrived at his brother's house, Gianni felt he might have finally absorbed the brunt of the shock. He rang the doorbell and waited for someone to answer, not even sure exactly how to break the news to Angelo. There was a lot to explain, given the circumstances.

His brother opened the door wearing pajama bottoms and a gray T-shirt that had seen better days. "Please tell me you're not here to rile my kids up right before bedtime."

"No. That's not why I'm here, though it's very likely to happen."

Angelo looked upward, whispering some kind of prayer to the deity above. "You gonna let me in, or what? It's starting to drizzle out here."

Angelo rubbed his jaw, as if thinking about leaving him out there. "I suppose I have to," he said as he walked inside, leaving Gianni to step in and shut the door behind him.

"Though you might be recruited to help with a bath and then to read a bedtime story. Don't say I didn't warn you."

Angelo continued walking toward the kitchen where Gemma could be heard demanding more water in her cup. Gino was nowhere to be seen or heard. Which, based on past experience, did not bode well for anyone.

"Well, that's part of the reason I'm here, little bro," he said to Angelo's back.

"Yeah, why's that?" Angelo asked, throwing the question over his shoulder. "You'll never convince me you actually came here to help with the bedtime routine."

"Ah, that's where you'd be wrong. See, it turns out I might need the practice."

It took an instant or so for his words to register. Angelo stopped in his tracks and whirled around to face him. "Come again? Why would you need practice—" Gianni watched as realization dawned over his brother's features. "Honey," he bellowed in the direction of the kitchen. "You might want to come out here."

"I just found out myself."

"Just found out what?" his sister-in-law wanted to know.

"Looks like our little *bambinos* are going to have a cousin soon."

Marie gasped and nearly let go of the toddler on her hip. Angelo strode across the room, his hand outstretched. Gripping Gianni's palm in his, he gave him a firm, hard handshake.

"Well, don't keep us in suspense. Who is the unlucky lady?"

If they only knew. "It happens to be a bit of a long story."

Marie pointed to him. "Then I suggest you brew some coffee, then come upstairs to help your brother and I get the little ones bathed and tucked in."

Gianni scoffed in mock affront. "You're so bossy."

His sister-in-law nodded. "*Si.* And I'm also nosy. So let's get to it. You know where the coffeepot is."

He'd have to brew it really strong. Telling them the entire story was going to take a while.

Forty-eight hours, forty-seven minutes and however many seconds.

That's how long it had been since she'd spoken with Gianni about her baby. *Their* baby. She hadn't heard a word from him since save for a couple of impersonal texts. No matter. Nothing he could say would make a difference at this point anyway. She was going to be a mother, and if that meant single parenthood, then so be it. She'd find a way to cope.

A small knock sounded at her office door and pulled her out of her thoughts. It had to be her cousin. Mabel was on a two-week break from school. She usually helped out at the club when she wasn't up in Vermont studying and she was here helping now. Thank the heavens for it too.

Laney was definitely slowing down, even though it was rather early in the first trimester. This little one was already proving to be rather demanding, between the increase in her calorie count and the sheer exhaustion she often felt.

"Come in."

She pulled the supply order form from under the pile of papers on her desk. Mabel had offered to do the weekly inventory for her. But the footsteps sounded wrong, too heavy. A lump formed in her throat when she looked up.

"Hey, Laney."

How many times in one lifetime could he approach her that way, completely unannounced? Each time felt as if a rug had been pulled out from underneath her.

"Hope it's okay to just show up?"

She did her best to appear unaffected. Inside, she was a shaky mess. "That depends, I guess. What exactly are you doing here?"

"I came to check up on you. Are you feeling all right?"

"I feel fine," she lied. He didn't need to know about the exhaustion or the sudden bout of morning sickness that had come out of nowhere and nearly had her heading back to bed.

"Good. That's good."

Leaning back in her chair, she folded her arms across her chest. "Was that it, then?"

He looked at her in question. "I'd say it's not. Don't you think we need to talk?"

"Oh. So now it's time to talk. No business meetings today, I take it?"

Without asking, he pulled the chair by the wall over and across from her desk and sat down. Laney had half a mind to tell him not to bother, but figured she owed it to her unborn child to hear him out. For now, at least.

"I apologize for that. I was not in exactly a good position to talk at that very moment. Not physically or in any other sense."

Did he think that served as any kind of acceptable excuse? She was convinced he wanted nothing to do with her or their child since she had barely heard from him aside from a few perfunctory text messages. Now, here he was telling her he thought they *needed to talk*.

She summoned a deep breath to try to calm down. Just last night, she'd read in her baby book that stress hormones could have an impact on the baby. It didn't help that he looked as handsome as ever. His hair had grown just enough that it almost reached his shoulders now. He must have been at the gym earlier. He had that glow that came from a good bout of exercise followed by a long shower.

She really had no business imagining him in

the shower. *Focus!* “And since then? It’s been almost three days since we spoke.”

“Didn’t you get my texts? Asking how you were?”

If he thought texts were adequate in this situation, he was sorely mistaken. “Texts? You think a few texts were enough?”

“Laney, I didn’t want to come and talk until I had everything in order. There were a lot of matters to tie up. Please know that I understand what a huge responsibility this is. One I don’t take lightly.”

There it was. Responsibility. Loose ends to tie up.

While she considered this baby a blessing to cherish, he clearly saw their situation as just an inconvenience that had to be addressed. Yet another rejection, another let down. Gianni no doubt planned to move on with his life. Who knew if she or their child would even be part of it. And she had no business feeling hurt or even surprised. Given what he’d told her that night on his aunt’s balcony, the complicated relationship he had with his parents, she knew it must be difficult for him to find himself an unplanned expectant father.

Still, it was pretty hard to accept. Without warning, her anger suddenly morphed into pure, unfiltered weariness. She didn’t have all the answers, and just felt so tired.

Another knock on her door suddenly interrupted them. It was followed by her cousin rushing into the room. "Sorry it took me so long. Had a little spill of pomegranate juice as I was mixing. What a mess. Red liquid everywhere!" She halted when she finally realized Laney had a visitor. Her eyes narrowed when she realized who that visitor was. "Gianni. Wish I could say it's nice to see you again."

He didn't acknowledge the goading nor the tone. Mabel had been the one to hear the alternating angry then sad rants since Laney returned from Europe. "Mabel. Hope you've been well," he answered with a polite nod in her direction.

"I can come back another time?" Mabel directed the question at her.

But Gianni answered by standing up. "I should be the one to go. Can we meet for dinner, Laney? To discuss all this and go over all our options."

He may as well have been speaking about a business negotiation. As much as she wanted to get it over with, delaying this conversation would give her time to get her thoughts together. "I think that's a wise plan."

"I'll see you in a couple of hours."

"Are you okay?" Mabel asked as soon as Gianni had left. "That was pretty intense."

"I'm not sure I'd describe things that way,"

Laney answered, waiting for her pulse to slow. Seeing Gianni for the first time since announcing her pregnancy was wreaking havoc on her insides. "I'd say Gianni was the opposite of intense just now."

"What do you mean?" Mabel asked.

Laney puffed out a sigh in frustration and pushed the bangs off her forehead. "He's just so… I don't know…flat, and straightforward. As if this is all no big deal." Darn it, her eyes were beginning to sting. She was not going to cry. Not again.

"You want him to be more excited about the baby."

That was it in a nutshell. Funny how she hadn't been able to articulate that one fact. Not even to herself, let alone be able to communicate it to Gianni. "Is that too much to ask?"

Mabel walked around the desk and sat on the edge of it, facing her. "Of course not, sweetie."

Laney sniffled, still desperately trying to keep the tears at bay. She wasn't sure how much longer she could hold out. "My parents could barely hide their disappointment in me. Again. That I'd gotten myself in yet another predicament they see as less than ideal." She squeezed her eyes shut at the memory of the heavy scene in her parents' living room when she'd broken the news to them. "Mom's first words after I told them was to ask how I could have been so careless."

Mabel's lips tightened. "I'm so sorry. As much as I love my aunt and uncle, they can be completely tone-deaf. They've always been the type that had that proverbial stick up their—"

Laney cut her off before she could complete that unseemly statement, as funny as it was. "Well, I seem to be the only one feeling any sense of thrill about this soon-to-be little human."

Mabel patted her arm. "That's not true. You know I can't wait to be an aunt to this little one."

"Thank you for that. I wish Emily had said the same thing when I told her yesterday."

"I take it she was also less than congratulatory."

"You would be correct. If I didn't know better, I'd say she was rather disappointed that I'd be a mother before her. She's the one who just got married."

"Families come in all different ways these days. Plenty of women have babies on their own."

"Yes, I know." Looked like she was well on her way to becoming one of those women. Life as a single parent was daunting, and she couldn't help but feel scared. But she'd do whatever it took to make sure her baby thrived. Having her child's father by her side, in some way or another, would have been ideal. But it didn't seem to be in the cards for her.

"And we both know Emily usually finds ways to feel slighted. She'll come around. And so will your parents."

But her family's reaction was secondary. What mattered more than any of their feelings about her child was the way the baby's father felt about him or her. Judging by what she'd seen so far, all indications implied he felt little to nothing.

"I hope so, May." She patted her belly. "Or else the size of our family is going to be small indeed."

CHAPTER FOURTEEN

MAYBE AGREEING TO dinner at Gianni's apartment hadn't been the best idea on her part. After all, this was where it had all begun. The night he'd cooked dinner for her seemed ages ago. Hard to believe it had been close to two months ago. How different things were between them now.

Laney sighed and pulled her car to park along the only spot left on the street. As she reached the steps, Gianni's door suddenly flew open and a small child ran out onto the porch. A little boy. He looked to be about two or three. The slight resemblance was there if one looked hard enough. He had to be Gianni's nephew.

"Hi!" he declared to her, then stuck his thumb in his mouth. Gianni stepped through the door at that very moment. He lifted the child up and in one smooth gesture lifted him over his head to sit on his shoulders.

Laney had to remind herself to breathe. The image of Gianni with a small child was pushing all the wrong buttons. If he had planned this scene, he couldn't have done a better job.

"Hey. You're here." He gave his nephew a small bounce on his shoulders. "I see you two have met."

She had to clear her throat in order to speak. "Um… We were just getting acquainted."

"Gino won't be here long. Angelo just ran out to get some groceries from the North End."

He motioned her in, then followed her through the door, ducking low as he entered. His nephew giggled when he finally let him down. The little boy scrambled away toward the living room where several wooden puzzles lay scattered across the rug. He bit down on one of the large pieces before trying to cram it into a spot it clearly didn't fit in.

"You're babysitting?"

"Yeah, sorry. He was supposed to be picked up an hour ago. Angelo's just running late."

"No. Don't apologize. I'm glad to be able to meet your nephew."

Gianni glanced at his watch. "Well, looks like you're going to be able to meet my brother, as well. He should be here any minute."

Laney was a grown professional woman. Yet the prospect of meeting Gianni's brother for the first time sent a shiver of nervousness down her spine. What would he think of her? What would his parents think when she eventually met them?

Though she hadn't allowed herself to really dwell on it, she had to acknowledge there might still be some lingering resentment about her unwillingness to sell her business.

All of that had to be water under the bridge, however. They had bigger fish to fry, as the saying went.

"The good news is my babysitting fee is being paid in a very valuable currency."

She had to laugh at the clear humor in his tone. Gianni's natural charm served well to lighten some of the tension. She couldn't help but feel appreciative. "What would that be?"

"Desanti's pizza. Extra-cheesy. Hope you're hungry."

How uncanny. She'd been craving pizza for the past day or so, never getting around to order any. Usually, by the time she got home, she was so famished and so low on energy that she nibbled on toast while boiling pasta or reheating leftovers.

"It's like you read my mind."

The doorbell sounded at that moment and whoever it was didn't bother to wait for an answer. A slight breeze blew through the room as the door opened and a tall wide-shouldered man carrying several large pizza boxes stepped through. The aroma of garlic and cheesy tomato immediately filled the air.

"There he is now," Gianni declared. "About time, little bro. What took you so long? Come meet Laney."

Angelo left with his son about thirty minutes after walking in, taking two of the boxes of pizza with him. Laney had concluded right away that there'd never been any reason to feel anxious about meeting Gianni's younger sibling. The man had an easy demeanor and charming sense of humor. Plus, the teasing banter between the two brothers, where they incessantly and mockingly insulted each other, made for a rather humorous dinner.

And now she and Gianni were alone. No buffer in the form of an adorable toddler or a talkative distracting sibling. Time to acknowledge the real reason for this little visit.

Laney took a sip of her sparkling water, watching as Gianni tidied up the kitchen and loaded the dishwasher. How could a man look so sexy doing tedious housework? And the way he'd been with his nephew, playful and patient. He'd laughed and simply cleaned up when Gino launched a slice of pizza across the table, splattering sauce and cheese everywhere.

Yeah, it was pretty clear Gianni Martino

would make an excellent father, if he only wanted to. That was the part that wasn't quite clear from where she was standing.

He joined her in the living room after drying his hands on a dish towel. "Did you get enough to eat?"

"More than enough. I might have had one full box."

"Hardly counts. You only ate from the plain cheese."

She rubbed a hand along her very full middle. "My tummy definitely disagrees with you. Trust me, it counts."

Gianni chuckled, then turned serious in a rather striking transformation. Looked like it was time to stop avoiding the elephant in the room.

"Listen, Laney." He braced his elbows on his knees and leaned toward her. "I just want to tell you that I take full responsibility for what's happening."

His statement sounded perilously close to an apology. She wasn't having it. "I played a fairly significant role in getting us to this point also, Gianni." After all, she'd been the one to invite him back to the hotel that night after the harbor cruise. Then she'd asked him to stay with her all night. "I was the one who did the asking that night, remember?"

He shrugged. "I wasn't exactly resisting."

There was no point in any of this. So much was being left unsaid while they tiptoed around useless niceties. But darned if she knew how to push past the formality between them now. In many ways, Gianni's demeanor at the moment reminded her of the time he'd shown up at her office to finally admit that he'd been planning on making her a business offer all along. This wasn't the warm, charming man who accompanied her around Positano, then took her to his beloved aunt's house, where he sat with her on the balcony, laying bare his soul. And it most definitely wasn't the passionate and sensual man who had spent the night with her in Boston.

She didn't know how to breach the distance to Gianni Martino in his current alteration.

"You should know I've already started the process of setting up both trust and college funds." She'd expected as much. "I can send you the files with details on all the portfolios," he added.

She shook her head. "That won't be necessary. I trust you know what you're doing. I'll be making my own investments."

"Fair enough. And, of course, I will contribute to day-to-day expenses. I have my accountants sending you documents as we speak."

A muscle twitched along his jaw before he spoke again. His shoulders visibly tensed. "As far as my role, I want you to know that I'll respect your discretion. To a point."

Okay. "What does that mean?"

"I'd like to be a part of this child's life. I'm willing to be flexible, and I'll bend over backward to make sure you're completely comfortable with my level of involvement. But I do plan to be involved."

"I understand." What kind of woman did he think she was? Of course, she had no intention of keeping him from his child. If anything, the more likely possibility was that eventually he would see both her and the child as more of a remnant from a past life.

He'd been so clear and adamant about not wanting a family. Or children of his own. He was saying all the right things now but would he eventually grow resentful that one had been forced on him and turn his back on her and their child?

Pain seared through her chest at that very real possibility. Then she'd have the Herculean task of making sure her child remained sound and whole afterward. Maybe it was the hormones, but the thought of her baby's father simply moving on with his life and leaving them behind as the unintended consequences from his past fling felt like a gut punch. It took all she had not to double over.

"I can have paperwork drawn up which outlines specific details if you like." He was back to being all business again. Not that he'd ever completely stopped.

"I don't think that's necessary. But go ahead if it makes you feel more comfortable, Gianni."

He leaned back against the couch, rubbed his jaw. "There is one other option I feel we should consider."

"And that is?"

"We could always get married."

Laney stared at him as if he'd grown horns atop his head. She gave a brisk shake of her head before speaking. "I'm sorry. I could have sworn you said we might want to consider getting married. I'm sure I must have misheard."

She looked so cute when she was taken aback. Clearly, she hadn't been expecting such a suggestion in the least. But it made sense, even if it was a rather unconventional marriage proposal. He'd thought about it over and over and kept coming to the same conclusion. Despite how he felt about the so-called sanctity of marriage, there was more at play here. He wanted his son or daughter to feel accepted and loved. He wanted this baby to know exactly who they were and who their parents were. If Gianni had his way, his child could grow up in a home with two loving parents. Legally, all the red tape and financial issues would be so much easier to address. Why have a child grow up in a broken home if there was an alternative? All logical. "That is indeed what I said."

Laney cupped her hand to her mouth and chuckled. "Right. Ha-ha."

She thought he was joking. "Laney, I'm being serious. Think about all the ways it makes sense."

Dropping her hand, she slowly shook her head. "You and I know it only makes sense for one reason. The only reason you're even suggesting it. You're only doing this because I'm pregnant."

"I can think of worse reasons for a couple to tie the knot."

She suddenly stood, waving her arm in clear frustration. "You wouldn't have even considered getting married if we didn't find ourselves in this predicament. Why would you change your mind?"

He would have thought that was obvious. "I think you know why."

Her shoulders suddenly slumped. "This isn't the middle ages, Gianni. Couples who are expecting together are perfectly capable of co-parenting without tying themselves down to each other forever through marriage."

Ouch. Quite a strike to his ego. The thought of marriage to him was obviously not a palatable one for Laney Taytum. Not that it should surprise him, anyway. Her thinking made sense. They had nothing in common. He knew full well she was in a completely different league. A much higher one. Still, there was a child to consider now. It wasn't about just the two of them.

"First of all, marriages don't always have to be based on some kind of emotion. Lots of unions are made simply because they're beneficial for both parties."

Something shifted behind her eyes. "I'd like to think mine will mean more than that. Or at least I plan on approaching my own marriage that way."

He didn't voice out loud what he was thinking. Unlike him, Laney appeared to harbor the illusion that love and affection had to be the impetus behind a proposal of marriage. He had no such delusion. "Look, I'm simply putting forth all our options. I think we should be open-minded, that's all. Just give it some thought."

She crossed her arms in front of her chest, studied him up and down. "You really are serious."

He stood too, strode over to her across the room and gently lifted her chin. "Think about it, Laney. We tend to get along for the most part. Think of all the fun we had together in Italy. The spark between us the night we met." He didn't imagine the way her body shuddered. She knew what he said was the truth, so he pushed further. "We certainly seem to be compatible in bed."

Her lower lip quivered and it took all he had not to lean down and take that lip with his own, to kiss her until that strained, incredulous expression melted off her face and all she could think about was just how compatible they'd been. Not the time.

"That's hardly a foundation upon which to start a marriage," she argued.

He dropped his hand from her chin. "Maybe. But it's a fairly strong start, I'd say. More than what a lot of couples have."

Couples like his parents for instance. What good was their intense love for each other when the very crux of their relationship depended on one big lie?

Of all the ways she'd imagined being proposed to—on a whirlwind trip through Italy, over a romantic dinner, maybe during a lazy stroll through gentle waves along a Cape Cod beach—that it might happen sitting in a living room in South Boston amidst a clutter of wooden preschool puzzles hadn't occurred to her once.

"Please don't answer right away. I want you to give it some real thought. In a logical and responsible way."

There was that word again. *Responsible.*

He really thought she might be able to accept a marriage proposal that had only been offered out of a sense of duty. Simply gravy or icing on the cake that they happened to be physically drawn to each other. It was all so wrong.

There was no point in telling Gianni, but she already knew her answer. She'd been living in a loveless family her whole life. She had no intention of starting her own family with a loveless marriage. Especially given that even the mere potential for developing any kind of love was completely one-sided.

The word hadn't so much as crossed Gianni's lips.

"What exactly did you have in mind?" she asked, genuinely curious about just how much thought he'd even given this whole suggestion. "That we find a justice of the peace, sign some papers and then be off on our way?"

He gave a slight shrug of his shoulders. "That seems to be the most feasible way."

He really hadn't given this much thought at all. He was asking her practically on a whim.

He rubbed his jaw. "If it's the thought of missing out on a wedding that you're concerned about, I'm sure we can think of a way to throw some kind of party."

He thought she was worried about a lack of

celebration behind their mock nuptials. Granted, they hadn't met that long ago but she'd really thought he knew her better. That did it. For such a smart, successful man, he certainly could be rather clueless. She began to turn on her heel, at a complete loss for words when he gently took her by the forearm.

"Whatever you decide, it won't change anything else we talked about. I plan on being a father to this child in every way that matters."

At least there was that.

"You can be as involved in his or her life as you want to be," she reassured him. "I promise you that."

"Thank you," he said simply. "Just promise me you'll think about it. Getting married."

That much was an easy promise to make. No doubt, she wouldn't be able to think of much else. She could only nod in response.

Gianni knew he had to give her time and some space. But it was really hard to focus on any kind of business—or anything else, for that matter. He'd been so distracted in the ring while sparring this morning he'd failed to duck a powerful right hook and currently sported a nasty bruise right below his cheekbone.

Laney wasn't exactly ignoring him; she responded right away to his texts and calls. But her answers were short and to the point. Bordering on curt. He had no idea if she'd given his proposal any thought whatsoever. It had been close to a week. Maybe the length of time was answer enough in itself.

He picked up his phone with the intention of calling her for the umpteenth time that afternoon only to slip it back into his pocket. He didn't want to pressure her in any way. But the truth was, he had to admit he missed her. An hour didn't go by where he didn't think about her and how she must be doing. Was their baby okay? Was she getting enough to eat?

Weren't pregnant women supposed to be taking some kind of vitamin regularly? He needed to be sure to ask her about that at some point. In fact, he could do so right now. For his own piece of mind, if nothing else. He pulled his phone back out and this time actually clicked on her number.

She answered but not until so many rings passed that he was convinced he was about to land in her voice mail.

"Hi, Gianni. Sorry, I almost didn't hear the phone. It's really loud here."

"Where are you?" And what was all that shrieking in the background? It sounded like she could be in the middle of a rowdy soccer match.

She chuckled softly into the phone. He barely

heard it. "Impromptu trip to the aquarium. Mabel had some research she needed to do before returning to school. Asked me to come along." That explained all the noise.

"Sounds very busy."

"There appear to be at least three different school field trips."

"Does that mean you're having fun?"

"Yes and no. Mabel's been in the lab for about an hour now. At the moment, I'm admiring the jellyfish exhibit by myself."

He heard the shriek of a child in the background. Or maybe it was several shrieking children, he couldn't even tell. He couldn't remember the last time he'd visited the aquarium but he certainly remembered how loud it had been while he was there. And also the headache he'd been burdened with afterward. So he surprised himself when he asked her the next question.

"I'm not too far from there. Want some company?"

She paused so long that he peeked at the screen to make sure the call hadn't disconnected somehow. When she finally answered, he could hardly hear for all the noise.

"Sure. Why not? I'll probably have moved on to the penguins by then. I'll see you in a bit." With that, she disconnected the call.

Less than half an hour later, that's exactly where he found her. Leaning up against the rail, staring at the variety of penguins in the faux Arctic below. A group of schoolchildren rushed by them, two very harried looking chaperones fast on their heels. Aside from the crowds and the noise, Gianni remembered the other thing he didn't enjoy about the aquarium—the aroma in this particular area of the building.

"Cute little guys, aren't they?" he said, reaching her side. "If you can ignore the smell."

She tapped the informational plaque in front of them. "It says here some penguin species mate for life."

They'd be the select few. He wondered if any of the penguin pairs ever cheated. The ridiculousness of the question had him chuckling out loud.

"What's so funny?" Laney wanted to know.

"Just penguins in general, I guess," he hedged.

She narrowed her eyes at him. "What happened to your face?"

Gianni touched a finger to the bruise on his cheek. "Nothing. Just a hazard of my sport of choice. It'll be fine."

She studied him some more but made no further comment. "Right. Should we head over to the central tank? They just announced it was feeding time."

That he could handle. The central tank contained large sea turtles and a few sharks. He gently took her by the elbow and led her to the circular ramp that wrapped around the Giant Ocean Tank in the middle of the building that towered over four stories. They stopped to admire a school of zebra fish that swam near the glass.

Crowds of children bustled by them. Hard to believe that in just a few short years he'd have a school-aged child himself. He imagined visiting a place like this, the wonder it would hold for a child seeing it for the first time. The picture in his head included the woman next to him. What that meant exactly he didn't want to examine too closely. But a nagging sensation told him he wasn't going to be able to ignore the implication behind it much longer.

They reached the top of the tank just as an aquarist in full scuba gear lowered herself into the water with a bucket full of fish feed. Unbelievably, the crowds were even thicker up here. How was the place so busy in the middle of the week? They were jostled more than once. Laney didn't seem to mind. Though she'd definitely slowed down as they reached the higher floors. He couldn't begin to imagine the toll pregnancy must take on a woman's body.

Laney turned suddenly to catch him staring at her. "What is it?"

“Nothing. Just admiring you as you admire the sea life.”

She blew out a long breath. “You shouldn’t say things like that to me, Gianni.”

Before he could respond to ask why, she’d already turned on her heel and was heading back toward the ramp. “I think I’d like to go pet the starfish and rays now.”

The petting area was all the way back on the first floor and was nowhere near as interesting. But he wasn’t going to argue. With a resigned sigh, he turned to follow her just as a small toddler ran smack into Laney’s thighs nearly toppling her over. Gianni reached her side just in time to catch her before she tripped over the child.

“I’m so sorry!” A harried-looking woman with a large backpack took hold of the little girl. “She moves so fast sometimes.”

“It’s all right,” Laney responded with a weak smile.

“Thanks for the catch,” she said after the mom and tot had left, not moving out of his hold. Was it his imagination or had she gone quite pale suddenly? The circles under her eyes grew darker and her lips appeared to turn blue.

Something was very wrong.

Her next words confirmed it. “I don’t feel too well all of a sudden.” She barely got the last word out as she slumped against him.

* * *

Laney's vision turned black just as her knees went weak. Thank heavens Gianni was there. She felt him gently lift her up and carry her to a bench against the wall.

"Laney? Honey?" Gianni's voice reached her ears as an echo. "I want you to try to take a really deep breath and then do it again and again. Can you try for me?"

She did her best to follow his direction. It seemed to help, if only a little. She managed to find her voice enough to make an attempt at telling him what she needed him to do for her.

"My OB. Contact. My phone."

Through the fog clouding her brain, she realized her attempts had worked. She felt Gianni reach into her cross-body pocketbook and pull out her cell phone.

"They have an office at Mass General," she heard him say.

Yes! He knew what to do. With the relief that realization brought, Laney continued to try to breathe as Gianni had instructed. As if observing through a tunnel, she felt herself being carried out of the building and into one of the taxis that always loitered around the harbor side.

She had no idea how much time had gone by when she opened her eyes to find herself lying on a hospital cot in a sterile brightly lit room with an IV in her arm. Gianni sat next to her, holding her hand.

"Guess I picked a rather inconvenient time to take a nap, huh?"

Gianni's head snapped up. He smiled at her. "Hey there, sleeping beauty. How do you feel?" he asked in a soft, gentle voice.

"Right now, I feel rather lucky that you were at the aquarium with me. Does Mabel know where we are?"

"I took the liberty of texting her after finding her contact information on your phone. I just told her you were with me. Not to look for you."

Not only had he caught her fall and rushed her to get help, he'd thought to notify her cousin so Mabel wouldn't be roaming the aquarium looking for her in vain. Gianni Martino really knew how to come through in a crisis.

A knock on the door preceded the entrance of her regular OB doctor. Laney shifted to try to sit up but then gave up given the effort it took. "Hey, Dr. Zhao."

"Hello, there," the petite woman with the sensible top bun greeted her, then took Laney's wrist to check her pulse. "Feeling better?"

"Yes. But I'm scared, to be perfectly honest. Is the baby…?" She couldn't complete the sentence. An icy dread of fear ran through her veins at even the possibility that something may have happened to her child.

"The baby appears to be fine." She lifted her stethoscope. "Strong and steady heartbeat."

The relief that surged through Laney's core had her shaking. Thank the heavens. Gianni's grip on her hand tightened and she heard his audible sigh.

Their baby was okay. "What happened?" she asked the doctor through dry lips.

"All signs indicate that you were simply dehydrated," Dr. Zhao answered. "The IV is taking care of that right now. Your vitals are good. Getting better as the fluid does its thing."

"Thank you." Laney felt the tear that had built up in her one eye slowly roll down her cheek.

"We're just going to keep you here for a while longer, about half an hour or so. Just for observation."

That sounded fine with her. It would take her about that long to recover from the scare alone.

Dr. Zhao continued, "I'm going to have Tina come in and strap a Doppler on you, so we can listen to the fetal heartbeat before we let you go. Just to be on the safe side." She pulled out a notepad from her lab-coat pocket and started scribbling. "I'm writing down the sports drinks I recommend. Of course, water works just as well. Just make sure to keep drinking. And I'd like you to come back in a couple of days. Just to follow up."

Laney wanted to hug the other woman. How could she have let herself get dehydrated? She could have really gotten hurt back there at the aquarium. If Gianni hadn't been there to catch her, she could have easily fallen and hit her head.

Gianni. She looked over at him as the doctor left. He looked visibly shaken. She'd given them both quite a fright. Any doubt she may have had about whether he cared about this baby was now soundly put to rest. If only she could be as sure he cared for her, as well.

"I'm really sorry," she told him as yet another tear fell.

He rubbed her cheek with the back of his hand. "Hey, you have nothing to apologize for. Well, maybe except for making me hang out in the smelly penguin exhibit for so long."

She managed a small smile at his lame attempt at humor. "Sorry about that, certainly. And also for scaring you."

He gently tussled her hair. "All that matters is that you and the little one are all right, *cara*."

The endearment hovered in the air between them. He hadn't called her that since Italy. The physician's assistant chose that moment to knock and enter. She pushed a cart into the room as she greeted them.

With an impressive efficiency and hands that were rather cold, the other woman wrapped a strap around her middle. She hooked the other end up to a rather archaic-looking machine.

Laney held her breath until the machine came to life. Then the steady singsong sound of her baby's heartbeat rang through the air. It had to be the sweetest rhythm she'd ever heard.

As the PA left, she looked up to find Gianni staring at her in wonder. Without a word, he walked over to her bedside and gave her a soft and gentle kiss on the lips.

CHAPTER FIFTEEN

GIANNI DIDN'T KNOW whether to jump up in joy or sink down into the floor. The past hour or so had been the most harrowing of his lifetime. His nerves had been shot, his every muscle tight with apprehension until he'd heard the doctor's reassurance. Then he'd felt the flood of relief in every cell of his body.

Now, listening to his baby's heartbeat as it sounded through the air was an experience he couldn't compare to any other. He'd known he wanted this child from the moment Laney called him that day at his accountant's office. But he hadn't realized just how much until the real fear that something might go wrong.

What a punch to the gut.

And Laney, he had to make sure she was better taken care of. From this moment, he was going to do everything he could to ensure it. If that meant finding a way to be with her more often, then so be it. Starting today.

"You don't have to stay, you know," she said

to him, lifting the top part of the bed using the controller. “I’m feeling much better now. I can find my way home.”

As if he’d leave her side. Not for anything in this world. Besides, he may never tire of listening to the steady thud of his child’s heartbeat. The sound of it brought home just how real all of this was. In a way that hadn’t hit him before. “You’re not getting rid of me. Don’t even think about it.”

She smiled, and the desire to walk over and kiss her, really kiss her this time—not some chaste little peck on the lips—had him clenching his fists to resist the urge. He was relieved to see she did indeed look much better. The color had returned to her face, her lips no longer a frightening shade of blue. He was going to run out and buy her cases and cases of sports drinks as soon as he had the chance.

“In fact,” he added, “I’d like to come back with you to the appointment.”

She looked ready to argue, then appeared to change her mind. “You know what? I’d like that.”

The half hour went by quicker than he would have thought. Gianni secured another cab while Laney made her appointment at the front desk.

“Are you warm enough?” he asked. “I can ask the driver to turn the heat up.”

“Gianni, it’s about ninety degrees outside.”

"Then I'll ask him to turn his AC down."

"I'm not cold. But thank you. And you didn't have to ride with me to my place."

She really didn't get it. He wasn't merely seeing her home. He intended to stay with her as long as she would let him. "I told you back at the hospital, I'm not leaving your side."

She gave a small shrug. "Suit yourself. But I don't plan on doing anything but taking a long hot shower and then crawling into bed for the longest nap I've ever taken." She accented the statement with a wide yawn and a long stretch of her lower back.

"I'm afraid not. That won't work."

"Come again?"

"First we're going to make sure you get something to eat. You missed lunch. We just got you hydrated. I won't risk malnutrition."

She laughed loud enough that it echoed through the back seat. "I'm hardly starving. But you're right. I could eat. My exhaustion was just winning out over my hunger."

"Do you have enough food in your apartment?"

"You know, you would have made a good nurse."

"I can think of a few people I'd like to jab with a needle from time to time."

She chuckled again and he realized, not for the first time, just how much he enjoyed her laughter.

* * *

She must have given him an even bigger scare than she thought. After setting her up on the sofa and covering her up with a plush afghan, Gianni was in the kitchen throwing together what he called a *satisfying, nutritious lunch* that both she and the baby would enjoy.'

It was so hard to keep her eyes open but the aroma coming from the kitchen was definitely an incentive to stay awake.

"You know, you don't have as much food here as you led me to believe."

She knew she had plenty. Just not enough that might satisfy a healthy Italian male who worked out regularly by throwing and receiving punches.

"I have all the basics."

"Life is about more than just the basics, *cara*."

There it was again, that word. Dear, beloved.

She knew she couldn't look too deeply into the endearment. It was just an expression…one he probably didn't even realize he was using.

Gianni walked into the living room a few minutes later, carrying a tray he set down on the coffee table in front of her. Her mouth watered at the sight of the food. He'd made an omelet that was so loaded it was overflowing at the fold. Next to the plate sat a perfectly browned piece of toast slathered in so much butter it looked downright wet. A tall glass of water with lemon wedges had just the amount of ice cubes she liked.

"Aren't you having anything? I could share—"

He didn't even let her finish. "That's all yours. You need to eat. I had a sandwich as I cooked."

Laney gave him a serious military-type salute and picked up the fork. "Yes, sir."

A burst of flavor exploded on her tongue as soon as she took a bite. Cheese, vegetables, myriad spices she wasn't even aware she owned.

The man was an artist. A girl could get used to this. But that was the whole problem in a nutshell. It would be all too easy to get used to having Gianni Martino around.

She thought of the look on his face when she'd first woken up in the hospital, the way he'd held her hand and squeezed it tighter as the doctor had walked in. Just the source of comfort and strength he'd been for her when she'd faced her deepest fear.

There was no denying it. She was falling for him. Head over heels, impossible to deny, tumbling with no hope of righting herself.

If only the man in question felt the same way in return.

Gianni lifted the tray off Laney's lap when she was finished and carried it back to the kitchenette of her apartment. "I believe you've earned your nap now, madame," he told her upon his return. It was clear she was struggling to keep her eyes open.

"I have one phone call to make and then it's off to dreamland I go for the next few hours."

"What's this important phone call? Anything I can take care of for you?"

She shook her head. "I need to call the club and let my manager know I'm not going to make it in tonight."

What he would have preferred to hear was that she would be telling them she didn't plan on making tonight, tomorrow and for the foreseeable future. But that was probably too much to ask. At this point in time, anyway. "Will that leave them shorthanded?"

"I don't think so. We shouldn't be that busy with two major concerts in town."

He sat down next to her as she reached for her phone, waited while she made the call and finally hung up. "All taken care of."

"For now."

"Yes. I'll eventually have to do more hiring. Especially once all the college kids head back to school. I have several working for me over the summer who won't be around much longer."

A tendril of apprehension curled through his middle. After the scare today, he didn't want to think about Laney overdoing it and risking her or the baby's health. Owning and operating any business took a lot of time and effort, let alone a popular nightclub like the Carpe D.

"Don't you think that's a problem?" he asked her. "Finding qualified service workers is tough enough under the best of circumstances."

"I'll have to move quickly to hire and get them trained. But I do still have several months."

He stood and started to pace the room. He couldn't believe how blasé she was being about this. "What happens when the baby gets here?"

She shifted and tucked her knees underneath her. "Well, for one, I plan on taking some time off, obviously."

"And then what?"

"Then there are several very reputable nanny agencies in the area."

He didn't want to overstep. But it was a fair subject. He had to know her exact plans moving forward. The baby was his too, after all.

"You plan to continue as is, then? You don't feel anything needs to change until the baby is born?"

"I don't think I follow where you're going with this."

"I would hate to have another replay of this afternoon. You can't let yourself get run down. Nothing matters but taking care of yourself now."

She tilted her head and gave him a questioning smile. "I was only dehydrated, Gianni. And my doctor is making sure to monitor me closely. You heard her yourself."

"I still think you should slow down. Take it a bit easier now that you're expecting."

There was one obvious way to do just that. She could go ahead and sell to his father. He knew firsthand what a lucrative offer was waiting for her if she only cared to look. Even if Gianni himself had walked away from the whole fiasco out of respect for her wishes. But that was then. Everything was different now. There was a child to consider.

And if she took him up on his marriage proposal, she could devote all her time in preparation of the upcoming birth.

"I can tell you have something you want to say, Gianni. Go ahead and say it, please."

Despite the question, her tone told him she wasn't ready to hear any of it. He had to pick a better moment. "It can wait. You've had enough of a day already. We'll talk some other time."

She sat up straighter. "No, I'd rather get it out in the open."

"Don't you want to take your nap?"

"I find I'm not all that sleepy anymore."

Rubbing a hand down his face, he tried to summon the right words to make his argument. Marrying him and taking his father up on the sale offer was the ideal solution to their current scenario. When the time was right, he'd do all he could to help her open up again elsewhere. With a club that was newer and better.

"All right, if you insist." He walked over and sat on the coffee table in front of her. "You still have an option you might not have considered."

Her eyes narrowed on him in suspicion. "What would that be?"

"You can still sell. My father's offer stands."

She sucked in a sharp breath. "I see. I take it that's what you would recommend I do, then."

"It makes sense, Laney. It would give you time to adjust to the new reality and get ready for the baby. Think about not having to worry about staffing, or drink orders or handling large crowds. You could just relax and focus on our child."

"So you're trying to convince me to sell because you're concerned about our child?"

He nodded. "Of course. And out of concern for you, as well."

"And that's the only reason? Your *concern* for us?"

The way she emphasized the word sent warning bells ringing through his head. "Why else?"

"Perhaps you could tell me."

For a moment, he was simply confused at what she was getting at. But then realization dawned and he couldn't believe what she suspected. Exactly how little did she think of him? "You think I'm telling you this in order to acquire a building?"

Her lips tightened before she answered, "Aren't you? Isn't there a well-known theory that says the most obvious conclusion is usually the correct one?" She pushed her bangs off her forehead. "I can't believe I've been so naive."

"Laney. You can't possibly think I don't have your best interests at heart here. Yours and the baby's."

But she didn't even appear to be listening. Her jaw suddenly dropped and she stared at him, her mouth agape. "Oh, my God. Is that the only reason you proposed? How nice and tidy. You get legal rights as a father…your family's business gets the property they've been after."

"What? Of course not!" How could she even think such a thing, let alone voice it out loud?

"It's so clear from where I'm standing."

Her doorbell rang before he could respond. Without a word to him, Laney threw the afghan off and went to answer it. Her cousin Mabel stood across the threshold. She threw her arms around Laney and the two women embraced in a tight hug. "I came to check on you after getting your text. Are you okay now?"

Apparently, Laney had filled Mabel in about the afternoon's events at some point.

As he watched the two women, Gianni felt the muscles of his jaw clench in frustration and disappointment. Along with another hollow feeling he didn't want to label—the only word that came to mind was *hurt*. How little credit she gave him. She just assumed the worst of him. At this very moment, he had documents and proposals being drawn in order to walk away from the family business once and for all. A decision he'd made in no small part because of how she'd reacted that day he told her the truth.

The idea of marrying him and focusing on the family they could have together was so unappealing to Laney Taytum that she would rather believe he was trying to dupe her for a mere business deal.

It was just as well Mabel had arrived. For he couldn't stay. Not after what Laney had just accused him of. He had to get out of here.

With a short and somewhat terse goodbye to them both, he strode out the door.

Laney watched the door shut behind Gianni and heard his footsteps grow fainter and fainter as he walked away. For one insane moment, she wanted to run after him. To plead with him to come back and convince her that all the things she'd just said weren't true. To somehow prove her wrong.

Clearly, he couldn't do that. Or he wouldn't have taken off in the first place.

Well, so be it. She could do this all on her own. She knew in her heart that she was going to be a good parent, regardless of whether or not she had the child's father with her for any kind of support. This pregnancy and the events of the past few weeks had taught her one thing: she didn't need anyone else's validation to prove her worth. Not her parents' or even Gianni's.

So why had watching Gianni walk away hurt so sharply? How often could she be so naive when it came to one man? Here she was, once again wondering what exactly between them was real and how much of it was her simply being blind and gullible where he was concerned.

"He certainly left in a hurry," Mabel commented. "Hope it wasn't because of me."

Maybe it was the hormones, or maybe the harrowing events of this afternoon. Or maybe it was simply the toll their argument had taken. But Laney felt a wave of emotion so powerful crest through her core that it threatened to crash with a fierceness that made her tremble. The next thing she knew, she was sobbing in her cousin's arms.

"Laney. What is it? I thought you said you and the baby were okay."

Alarm and fear rang loud and clear in Mabel's voice. That just made Laney feel worse. "We are.

I'm sorry. I should be grateful for that fact alone. And I am. I really am."

Mabel led her over to sofa and sat her down, yanking a few tissues from the box on the counter along the way.

"Tell me," she coaxed. "And then I'll go get the mint chocolate chip from the freezer."

At her cousin's prompting, the words seemed to pour out of her in a torrent. Starting with Gianni's proposal a week ago, to the harrowing scare at the aquarium and ending with the ghastly conversation they'd just had, which led to him storming out the door with barely a goodbye. By the time she was done, her throat felt raw and sore and her breath came out in raspy gasps.

Mabel blew out a puff of air and handed her yet another tissue. "So, let me get this straight. The man flew all the way to Italy to apologize. He took care of you when you felt unwell. Then he pointed out to you that you had an option that would make it easier for you to take some time off during your first pregnancy. Before that, he asked you to marry him. And you were upset because he didn't do it the right way. So you accused him of trying to fool you into a sham business deal. Do I have all that straight?"

Well, when she put it that way. "He only proposed because he felt it was the right thing to do, Mabel. When and if I accept a marriage proposal, I don't want it to be out of a sense of duty. Maybe I'm being foolish, but I want it to be born of affection. Of love," she added on a hiccup that sounded pathetic to her own ears.

Mabel nodded with enthusiasm. "Oh, I definitely agree with you there."

"You do?"

"Absolutely. But there's one thing you don't seem to be taking in mind."

"What's that?"

"Consider everything you just told me. I'd say those were definitely the actions of a man in love."

Laney immediately began to protest, but an inkling of doubt began to sprout like a tiny seed. What if her cousin was right and she'd just made a colossal error? "That can't be. He's never so much as said anything to that effect."

Mabel shrugged. "Sometimes actions speak louder than words. And the fact is, he's done more than enough to show you he cares about you, coz."

Did Mabel have a point? A small voice in her head began to nag at her. The facts were that Gianni had agreed to pretend to be her real date for her sister's wedding, he'd flown across the world as a way to apologize to her after upsetting her and he'd been nothing but caring and attentive after finding out she was pregnant. And she'd simply discounted all of those deeds.

"Oh, dear. What if I've made a horrible mistake?"

"I'd say that's a distinct possibility." Mabel gave her arm an affectionate squeeze. "We're gonna need that ice cream."

Mistake. The word echoed around Laney's head and she knew she was simply making excuses for herself. What she'd done was more than a mere error. Rather than just tell him she hadn't changed her mind about selling her club, Laney had lashed out and accused him of selfishly trying to con her out of it.

She'd done it because she was afraid. So afraid of loving someone who might not love her back. Someone who might walk away from her and her child and leave her heartbroken and devastated.

So she'd lashed out. Because losing Gianni would undoubtedly shatter her.

And somehow, she'd probably just caused the very thing she feared.

CHAPTER SIXTEEN

Dad wants to see you.

ANGELO'S TEXT FLASHED on the screen of his smartphone as soon as Gianni arrived at his front door. Great. Just great. As if this day hadn't been enough of a nightmare already. To think, Gianni had only checked his phone in case it might be Laney reaching out. How foolish of him. She'd made it quite clear what she thought about his character.

His phone dinged once more. Angelo again.

Expecting you in his office sometime this afternoon.

The floating dots below the last message indicated there was more.

I wouldn't miss it if I were you.

Missing it was exactly what he wanted to do.

But he knew Angelo was right. The sooner he made his intentions clear to his father, the sooner he could move on. He would have his own child soon to focus on. He wanted everything squared away before the little one arrived.

Too bad part of the resolution wouldn't include this child being born into a family with two married parents. But that was overrated. That's what Laney had told him, anyway. She refused to marry him and she thought he was stringing her along for the sake of his family's company.

He cursed out loud as he unlocked his front door and threw his keys across the hallway, not caring that they hit the wall hard enough to leave a small mark in the paint.

He needed a good hour or two alone with a punching bag. Seeing his father was enough of a chore under the best of circumstances. When he told him what he intended, Gianni had no doubt all hell would break loose.

Oddly, he could hardly find the will to care.

Two hours later, after a punishing bout with the bag and a quick shower, he made his way to the building that housed Martino Entertainment Enterprises in Boston's Back Bay.

His brother was there when he reached the top floor and entered Franco's office. Angelo stood immediately and headed to the door. "I'll leave you two to it, then."

"You're welcome to stay, Angelo. This concerns you too."

But his brother gave a brisk shake of his head. "Oh, no. I've got to be somewhere else. Anywhere else." He wasted no time walking out of the room.

Coward, Gianni wanted to shout to Angelo's retreating back as he left and shut the door behind him.

His father leaned back in his chair and motioned for him to sit. "Hello, son. How is your fiancée? And the baby?"

So they were to begin with niceties. "They're both fine. Thanks for asking. But she's not my fiancée. We have no intention of getting married." Not for lack of trying on his part, but his father didn't need to know that.

"I see. That's a shame. Of course, she'll always be family now."

"Of course." That much was certain. He knew his mom and dad well enough to be confident that neither would see his child as any different from Angelo's kids. For all their faults, he appreciated their loyalty. Even if his father's had come at a cost to him personally, the way he'd never felt as if he belonged.

But this was not the time. It was best to get right to the matter at hand. Gianni pulled out a chair and sat down, loosening his tie in the process.

"I'm glad you called me in to talk."

"Do you know why I did?" his father asked.

Now that the question had been asked, Gianni had to admit he wasn't quite sure. He knew why he needed to speak to his father. But why had Franco insisted on seeing him today?

His father took his silence as an answer. "I've been hearing rumors."

"What kind of rumors?"

"That you've made moves to try and remove yourself as a VP of this company. That you're looking to buy the fitness division and run it independently."

He should have known Franco Martino would be one step ahead of him. He shouldn't have forgotten the wide network of associates and acquaintances Franco enjoyed. "I thought it might be prudent for me to take such steps."

His father waved an arm in dismissal. "You can't buy something you already own, son. This company belongs to you and your brother. I'm looking forward to retiring soon and traveling the world with your mother. She says she's tired of waiting."

Gianni would believe his dad was ready to retire when he saw it with his own eyes. But his mom was a strong woman; her influence with her husband was a force in itself. For all its trials and tribulations over the years, their marriage had somehow held. Gianni couldn't figure out how for the life of him.

Franco leaned over the desk, bracing his arms. "You are part of this family. You have had tremendous success growing the fitness and gyms branch of Martino Entertainment Enterprises."

He had to clear his throat before he could answer—a sudden lump of emotion had lodged at the bottom of his Adam's apple. "Thank you for saying that."

"Gianni, you are my son. Nothing will ever change that."

Gianni let the words sink in, fully and deeply. His whole life, he'd led himself to believe Franco tolerated him for the sake of the woman he loved. But maybe it was more than that. Maybe too much had been left unspoken until now.

Maybe his father had loved him all along. He'd just never been able to say it. "I understand, sir."

And he really did. Finally. Amazing the damage unspoken words could cause.

"Good," Franco said with a finality that made it clear he would say no more on the matter. "No more of this spin-off nonsense. Tell your lady she can hold on to her club if that's what she desires." He reached for the file lying on his desk and opened it. "Tell your brother to come back in here on your way out. I don't understand these numbers he's given me."

* * *

Gianni didn't bother to knock on his brother's door before strolling into his office. His mind was a jumbled-up mess. Between the revealing talk with his father just now and the heated conversation with Laney earlier, he felt disquieted and unsettled. For all the teasing and mocking insults between them, his brother had always been a good sounding board. Gianni figured he could use one of that right about now.

"When was the last time you bought me dinner?" he asked unceremoniously as he entered the room. "I'm feeling kind of hungry."

Angelo reached inside his desk drawer and pulled out a granola bar that he threw in Gianni's direction. He caught it with one hand and rolled his eyes.

"Never mind dinner," his brother said. "How did it go with the old man just now?"

"Fine. I think. I believe he just told me, in not so many words, that he cares for me."

Angelo scoffed. "That's it? You mean to tell me you two were having some sort of greeting-card moment? Here I thought it was something important."

His brother was doing all he could to make light of the situation, but Gianni could tell by his tone that both men realized the import of what had just transpired in their father's office. "He may have also saved me from pursuing an objective I didn't need to pursue after all."

Angelo lifted one eyebrow. "Yeah? Might this pursuit have had anything to do with the young lady who happens to be carrying your child?"

"It might. But it hardly matters now. We're having a disagreement about whether she should marry me or not."

"A disagreement, huh? What? She didn't like the ring or something?"

Gianni chuckled. "I never actually got her a ring. Wanted to see what she'd say first."

"You seem to have it backward, bro. Sounds like a pretty lame proposal. No wonder she disagrees."

"It's not like that. Not about the ring."

Angelo leaned back and crossed his arms in front of his chest. "I have no doubt it isn't."

"She just doesn't seem to want to see what's obvious."

His brother tilted his head. "What's so obvious?"

"That she and I make a good team. That we can parent this baby as a united couple. She doesn't realize that I happen to have fallen in—"

He stopped short. Whoa. Where had that thought come from? But he couldn't deny it. He loved Laney Taytum. He didn't even know when it had happened. He may have been well on his way the first night he met her.

"You need to tell her, bro," Angelo said. "The sooner the better."

His brother was right. He'd gone about it all wrong. How foolish and arrogant he must have sounded. Gianni had to let Laney know exactly how he felt. He had to tell her that he wanted to marry her because he loved her. And he had to ask her if she thought she might love him in return. Once and for all, they needed to get all of it out in the open.

He was through letting words left unspoken navigate the direction of his life.

Laney looked up in alarm as a car pulled up to the parking lot and Louise Miller got out. She was quickly followed by three others. The regular Saturday morning exercise crew. This was not good.

"Uh, Mabel? Did you forget to cancel the Zumba class? It looks like people are arriving ready to work out." Which would be a disaster. She was in no shape to do any kind of fitness instruction. Her recent bouts with morning sickness had had her knocked off her feet for a good part of the early day.

What she wouldn't give for a strong cup of coffee. She desperately missed caffeine and hadn't been sleeping well the past couple of nights. Ever since the momentous conversation with Gianni.

She had to find a way to say she was sorry. That she should have never doubted him. It was probably going to be the hardest apology she'd ever delivered.

But right now she had a more immediately pressing matter. Louise and the rest of the group were making their way inside. "Mabel?"

Mabel looked up from stacking the clean glasses behind the bar. "Oh, did I forget to mention? I was told not to cancel the class, after all."

That made no sense. "Who would have told you that?" And why would Mabel have taken direction from anyone but her? "I'm in no condition to run a Zumba class right now."

Mabel simply smiled at her. "Oh, I know. It's not Zumba. And you won't be running the class."

Before she could delve into that mystery, another familiar car pulled into the lot. Laney's heart did a somersault inside her chest when Gianni stepped out of the driver's side. Wearing sports shorts and a gray cotton T-shirt, he looked sexier than any man should dressed in simple shorts and a tee.

"Gianni's holding class today," Mabel explained behind her, as if that made any kind of sense.

"Why would he do that?"

"He called me last night. Said he wanted to help out a bit around here. We talked about what a shame it would be if you had to cancel your Saturday classes as the pregnancy progressed."

Laney wouldn't have been more surprised if Mabel had just told her that she'd purchased a unicorn and planned to go live with it in a castle in the clouds. Her jaw didn't seem to want to close.

"Gianni is going to teach an aerobics class to cover for me in my club?"

Mabel rolled her eyes. "Of course not. That would be silly."

Right. As if Laney was the one being silly right now. "He's going to teach a cardio kickboxing class, of course. I notified all the attendees who signed up about the change."

Sure enough, Gianni walked in a few seconds later with a sweat towel draped over his shoulder. As she watched, flabbergasted, he began the class with a warm-up routine, then continued for forty straight minutes with a pulse raising workout that had her regulars sweating. They all seemed to be enjoying themselves.

Herself included. She rather enjoyed watching him. He'd even thought to bring along a speaker with a pounding playlist to accompany the routine. At one point, he winked in her direction, making her blush like a schoolgirl.

At the end of the cooldown, after the attendees slowly trickled out, he made his way over to the bar where Laney still stood in mild shock. She had trouble making her mouth work. "You are full of surprises, aren't you?" she finally managed to utter.

"You haven't seen anything yet, sweetheart," he answered, leaning in to give her a peck on the cheek.

Heavens, she'd missed him. It had only been a few days but hardly a minute had gone by that she hadn't thought about him and how she might make things right between them. Now, here he was, after having run a kickboxing workout for her class, no less.

"You really plan on doing this every week?" she asked, for lack of a better conversation starter.

"You bet. I'm also taking bartending classes online."

"You are?"

He nodded. "I'll be around as often or as little as you want me to."

Laney rubbed her jaw, as if deep in thought. "I see. Well, I have to say, I've been doing some thinking since we last spoke, Mr. Martino."

"What kind of thinking?"

"Some of the things you said, about focusing on this pregnancy and my becoming a mom in a few short months. I've decided a lot of it has merit."

"What's that mean, exactly?" he wanted to know.

"It means, I've rethought your offer."

His smile slowly wilted. "Laney, you don't have to do that. I'm sorry I ever brought it up again. You don't have to sell. This place is your labor of love. We'll find a way to make it work."

She waved a hand in dismissal. "That's not the offer I'm referring to, silly man."

"It's not?"

"No. I mean the offer to marry you. Does it still stand? Because I'd like to say yes."

He blinked at her. Once, twice. In the next instant, she suddenly found herself lifted in his arms and spun around. When he finally set her down, he took her lips with his in a deep soul-shattering kiss she felt down to her toes. It took several deep breaths to get her oxygen level back to normal.

"I love you, Laney Taytum," he whispered against her ear in a tone so genuine that she felt the sting of joyful tears behind her eyes. "I was a fool not to tell you earlier."

She leaned in close against his chest, felt his arms tighten around her. "You did tell me. In so many ways. I just wasn't listening."

From now on, she would be all ears when it came to her soon-to-be husband.

"I love you," she, said against his chest, echoing his declaration. "And I can't wait for the three of us to be a family."

A family in which she truly felt she belonged.

EPILOGUE

"THE PHOTOS YOU sent are breathtaking!"

Mabel's excited voiced reached her through what sounded like an echo chamber. Laney strained to hear better over the crashing waves in the distance. It was a beautiful morning on the Amalfi Coast. The perfect day to enjoy the Marina Grande Beach.

"But please don't send me anymore," Mabel insisted. "I'm just about racked over with jealousy."

Laney sat up in her lounge chair to get a better view of Gianni and their baby girl splashing around in the water. The three of them had hiked the Path of the Gods yesterday, with Gianni carrying their daughter in a back carrier.

Laney had taken more snapshots than she could count, emailing more than a few to Mabel afterward. "Well, then you have to come here, Mabel. As soon as you get the chance. You'd like Gianni's cousin. He makes a mean limoncello."

Mabel giggled into the phone. "Are you playing matchmaker, coz?"

"Guilty as charged," Laney admitted. Would that be so wrong? Now that she had the family she'd dreamed about, Laney couldn't help but want to spread such happiness around. Her cousin more than deserved it.

"There's the small matter of a doctorate I need to finish up," Mabel reminded her.

"Fair enough," Laney agreed. "But after that's done, the next time we come here on holiday, I'm going to insist you come with us."

"It's a plan."

After they said their goodbyes and hung up, Laney grabbed the large plush Turkish towel sitting on the blanket next to her and approached the water where Gianni and their daughter were splashing around in the gentle waves. He held their precious child tight against his chest.

"All right, you two. You'll both start to prune if you don't come out right now," she chided. This was the third time she'd tried to get them to come out.

Her baby daughter's response was to kick her little feet in the water and send a toothless grin Laney's way. Not for the first time, Laney felt her heart swell with the love and joy that rushed through her whenever she looked upon her child.

"What do you think, Gia?" Her husband asked their little girl. "Is your *mamma* right? Should we get out?"

Of course, the eight-month-old didn't understand enough to answer. But Laney could have sworn she gave a subtle shake of her head.

"I agree," Gianni declared. "I think instead of us getting out, she should come in!"

In a stealth-like move she hadn't seen coming, he reached out with one hand to grab her by the arm and pulled her farther into the ocean with them. She barely managed to hold on to the towel, lifting it above her head so that it didn't get wet.

"Not fair," she teased, wrapping the towel safely around her shoulders to prevent it from falling. "The two of you are ganging up on me."

"Not true," Gianni argued. "You were simply outvoted."

Slipping his arm along her waist, he pulled her in closer against the length of him. For several moments, they simply stood in silence, with the gentle waves crashing along their legs and their daughter gurgling happily between them. Laney felt like pinching herself to make sure it was all real. Being here was a dream come true, with the man she loved and the beautiful family they'd created together.

She'd indeed found paradise.

* * * * *

If you enjoyed this story,
check out these other great reads from
Nina Singh

From Tropical Fling to Forever
Her Inconvenient Christmas Reunion
Spanish Tycoon's Convenient Bride
Her Billionaire Protector

All available now!